W9-BGW-961

Just a Face in the Dark

Books by Mark McShane:

THE STRAIGHT AND CROOKED
SEANCE ON A WET AFTERNOON
THE PASSING OF EVIL
UNTIMELY RIPPED
THE GIRL NOBODY KNOWS
NIGHT'S EVIL
THE WAY TO NOWHERE
THE CRIMSON MADNESS OF LITTLE DOOM
ILL MET BY A FISH SHOP ON GEORGE STREET
THE MAN WHO LEFT WELL ENOUGH
THE SINGULAR CASE OF THE MULTIPLE DEAD
THE HEADLESS SNOWMAN
SEANCE FOR TWO
THE OTHELLO COMPLEX
LASHED BUT NOT LEASHED
LIFETIME
THE HALCYON WAY

As "Marc Lovell":

THE IMITATION THIEVES
A PRESENCE IN THE HOUSE
THE GHOST OF MEGAN
ENQUIRY INTO THE EXISTENCE OF VAMPIRES
FOG SINISTER
DREAMERS IN A HAUNTED HOUSE
THE BLIND HYPNOTIST
THE GUARDIAN SPECTRE
THE SECOND VANETTI AFFAIR
A VOICE FROM THE LIVING
THE HOSTAGE GAME
AND THEY SAY YOU CAN'T BUY HAPPINESS
SHADOWS AND DARK PLACES
HAND OVER MIND
THE LAST SEANCE
THE SPY GAME
THE SPY WITH HIS HEAD IN THE CLOUDS
SPY ON THE RUN
APPLE SPY IN THE SKY
APPLE TO THE CORE
HOW GREEN WAS MY APPLE
ONE GOOD APPLE IN A BARREL OF SPIES
THE SPY WHO GOT HIS FEET WET
THE SPY WHO BARKED IN THE NIGHT
GOOD SPIES DON'T GROW ON TREES

Just a Face in the Dark

MARK McSHANE

PUBLISHED FOR THE CRIME CLUB
BY DOUBLEDAY & COMPANY, INC.
GARDEN CITY, NEW YORK
1987

All of the characters in this book
are fictitious, and any resemblance
to actual persons, living or dead,
is purely coincidental.

Library of Congress Cataloging-in-Publication Data

McShane, Mark, 1930–
Just a face in the dark.

I. Title.
PR6062.0853J8 1987 823′.914 87–6801
ISBN 0-385-24308-1

Printed in the United States of America
First Edition

Just a Face in the Dark

ONE

People meeting for the first time go out of their way to talk sense. This, unconsciously, is exposition. They are showing how they stand in respect to social values, politics, education, or any other aspect of themselves which they feel has to be exposed and offered for approval. The longer people know one another, the less sense they talk.

Years ago Jim and Elsie had stopped exchanging prolonged talk of any nature, except for the occasion dire. Mostly, they communicated by signs and sounds. If Jim blew out through pursed lips while stretching one arm, Elsie said for him to go ahead, a walk would do him good. When he hummed a snatch of hymn, she put down her crossword puzzle and went to fix coffee. Elsie's tongue-clucking meant she wouldn't mind strolling into the village for a drink, since stating so outright by folding the tablecloth could make Jim say he wouldn't give one thin dime to go out tonight.

Jim and Elsie Braddock had been married eleven years, eight of them spent here in Shank, an ageing art colony in the Appalachian peaks of northeast Georgia. Annually they went back to Ohio for a month, seeing family, wearing worldly smiles. All friends there from art-school days were into construction or insurance, committees or children. They looked contented and hale. To Jim it was a secret worry that he might not be envied as devoutly as he wished. Often, coming back to Shank, he was too despondent to be patronising with those who never went anywhere.

Another of Jim's secret worries, equalling his conviction that by the time he got cancer it would still be incurable, was the feeling that he had never become a high member of the Shank community. Despite the longevity of his stay, he felt himself to be viewed as a sideliner.

He was not, of course, classed as one of those who were called nobodies, Jim knew. Nor was he only midway up the scale, a contender. He was somewhere between there and the top, where reigned the majors.

That was the reason Jim had started getting involved with Missy, who was truly in as he saw it, a Shankite of consequence, one of the dozen real pillars among the remaining sixty-odd painters, composers, sculptors, and writers. A problem with the Missy situation was degree of secrecy: how to keep Elsie in absolute darkness while allowing everyone else to have the light.

Jim Braddock loved his wife. He did not, however, know it. He was unconscious of the fact that he had fallen in love with her that time she slanted her head to receive a kitten into the curve of her neck. Their marriage was one of those drift-into things, he thought. The boy who married the girl next door.

Jim didn't realise that he shuddered when Elsie cut herself in the kitchen, as she so often did. He didn't know how tenderly he held her when she came. He was unaware that the ache he got in his throat when she returned home late was for any other reason than he was getting ready to speak, to carp about her lateness.

It was to prevent the collapse of a comfortable partnership that Jim wanted his Missy doings kept out of Elsie's ken, Jim thought. Also it was because, like most husbands, he had always presented himself to his wife as unique, a man of honour—which had been true apart from the occasional bout with a female tourist. Jim had grown attached to that image of himself. Sometimes it made the inside of his nose tingle.

Except that the reality lacked charm, like living poor in a cottage, Jim Braddock's physical self formed a fair match for how he conceived of it. He was even honest about his paunch, in respect of existence if not mass. It, in any case, besides being not unusual on a man of thirty-three, was in keeping with the tallness, understated muscularity, and lazy drive. With a plump face that tried always to wear a good-guy smile, with sleepy eyes and hair as untidy as the verities in wine, Jim might have just gotten up in that cottage and been wondering whose breakfast he could take.

On this March evening he was standing by the hearth, a rock-built cavern in which a fire of damp logs hissed like a perverse villain. Behind him stretched the cabin's long main room. Floored in stone, topped by beams, it was as romantic as a sampler, convenient as a rival in love. The furniture smiled its comfort and the decor was the Braddocks' framed crayon drawings: hung, stood, and stacked.

"Yes, you ought to," Elsie said.

Unwilling, Jim left the fire. He walked down the room, looked into the kitchen, meanwhile telling himself Elsie couldn't possibly have known he had been thinking of getting away to see Missy. "Come again?"

"John Brown. You ought to go see him."

"And the poor guy just wants to be let alone?"

"It's the neighbourly thing to do," Elsie said as brightly as though she had never said it before. She was sitting at the table shelling peas.

Jim gave his left forearm a short, vigorous rub to change the subject. He was tired of the man who had moved into the next cabin but one month ago, a mystery seen close up by no one, including Store Marsha, who had acted as rental agent, by mail.

Ignoring the forearm signal Elsie said, "He's always hiding."

"Why not?" If John Brown wanted to keep himself invisible, going out only at night sometimes on his motor cycle, though never stopping in at the village, that was all right with Jim.

"His name's so phony," Elsie said. "Ask him for supper."

"He's probably got this horribly scarred face. Remember the Phantom of the Opera?"

"Nobody really wants to be a recluse."

After nodding all around the kitchen at his internal comment that lately they had been through many exchanges on this pattern, garrulous they were getting to be, Jim said, "I'll think about it. I'll spy out the ground."

"Tell him it's meatloaf," Elsie said.

Outside, still snuggling into his peajacket, Jim looked along the dirt lane. The three cabins, all on the right side, middle one in darkness, were as different as fingers of a shared hand, the fifty-foot gaps between a morbid untidiness of junk, logs, and household outcasts.

Or *The Picture of Dorian Gray*, Jim thought while telling himself that Min Kuzak was the rightful next-door neighbour, so she could call on Brown when she came for the summer.

What peeved Jim about the newcomer, in addition to all the attention he had been getting from the locals, was that he should be the one who was making approaches, not the reverse. There was the further danger of John Brown, his acquaintance made, becoming a clinger, one of those nobodies who stuck to you like stamps and reduced your potential.

However: the notion that his wife might consider him foolish for not making a simple approach to the stranger caused Jim to stamp his feet. He decided that after he had strolled up to the quarry and back, he would definitely knock on John Brown's door, if he didn't feel like walking the quarter mile into the village, where Missy might not be around anyway. That was that.

Shank was born one hundred years ago, housing for workers in quarries whose slate was in demand for roofing. What had been intended as the lower leg of a community that would climb still higher, following the excavations, stayed as the one and only due to competition from the wooden shingle. Shank, indeed, grew progressively smaller, like a retired politician. Out of annoyance at their Lord's lack of bounty, the workers burned the chapel down and put hymn books in outhouses. Finally, the quarries lost to the Depression.

Birth as an art colony came in the 1950s. A composer, wandering the nation to rest his mind and avoid an inspiring wife, arrived by error in Shank. He found that the picturesque log-and-stone cabins, most vacant, could be rented for a hum. An artist could surely manage without heating and supermarkets, laundromats and public transport, he reckoned, surely be uplifted by the pine-rich peaks that rose around the settlement like symphonies in green.

For two decades Shank offered sanctuary to the creative. One cabin became a bar-eatery and another expanded from handler of farm produce to general store, with more commercialism discouraged. Artists famous or struggling rejoiced that television reception was so bad and celebrated their escape from a reality which might have nurtured their gifts further.

The second dying of Shank began in the late seventies. Tourists came more often up the second-class hardtop, drawn by tales of wild parties, drugs, and some real way-out characters, the middle tale of which lush trinity had the most truth. While disappointed, people stayed on in hope. They happily quadrupled what the locals could afford in rents and in some cases bought. Prices rose, the poor departed. An oil giant threatened to put in a gas station. Amateur Bohemians came with their amateur talents, which, artists being even greater snobs than peasants, drove away the creative locals of national repute. Other people moved in because Shank, Georgia, was a risqué address. Like an innocent celebrity, the village was slowly being patronised to death.

Missy, one of those who didn't believe Shank was dying, perhaps due to the fact that she wouldn't know what to do with herself if die it did, had come three years ago to visit a friend. Staid Philadelphia would see her no more, she swore that first night, turning on under a minor poet. Shank had everything.

Missy loved the one-story cabins, which were as far from a high-rise as you could get, unless it was a hole in the ground. She relished the cunning store and the macho bar. She adored the accepted styles of loose hair and long dresses for women, beards and peajackets for men. She needed the feeling of family.

Especially, Missy loved being looked at by tourists and the locally square, who, she knew, saw her as the exotic creature she had been born to be and had determinedly become. She knew she was worth looking at with her dimply body, waist-nuzzling blond hair, and the face which turned from pretty to beautiful via summer's tan.

That Missy was over-familiar with her physical being,

like the blind, was from the hours she spent in front of a mirror, at practice for work. She modelled, posing nude. The degradation, she lyingly complained, had to be borne as a life support to enable her to write poetry. That, like a wheedler's smile, was another pretty lie, for the only writing she did was to a disinterested but solvent father.

The lies formed a vital part of Missy's image (so necessary in Shank), along with the blare of her skirts, her fringed shawls, and the fact that her blouses were always buttoned incorrectly, so that top and bottom lay uneven. The first time she had misbuttoned this way, purposely, inspired, she had blushed on her neck. Nowadays she only smiled at her reflection fondly.

"I don't have a care in the world," Missy often said. But, like folk who protest that they are far from perfect, she didn't mean it.

It was less that she was twenty-seven years old than that by this age she should have made her mark, meaning become an outstanding personality in Shank, a major. She had not. As would be a human corpse in a butcher shop, she was an attraction without being attractive, wanted and sought out, not in respect of the majors. This she had bravely acknowledged but recently, though the suspicion had been hovering pimplike for some time.

Tourists and nobodies, they were thrilled to be permitted to talk with the exotic Shankite, but being seen with these people put you down as uncool yourself. It was worse if you let them stand you a drink, awful if they bought you a meal, offensive if you took one of them home for the night. All these anomalies Missy had committed. She couldn't help it. She loved the worship.

It was to abnegate such past mistakes and forge her way to the top that Missy now loitered beside the store. From inside came the cheery voice of Store Marsha (there was a

Weaver Marsha and once there had been a Painter Marsha). The storekeep was so in, so firmly a major, that neophytes were wont to show the tips of their tongues if she greeted them familiarly. Only by a real effort of will did Missy refrain from despising Store Marsha for being unaware of her power.

Opposite where Missy stood, across the hardtop and beside the chapel lot, was the village bar, called Gustav's, though no one could recall anybody of that name. What old-timers could recall was the furore caused when one of the ever-changing owners added the fronting stoop with its cover of corrugated tin. The question of convenience versus esthetics raged throughout construction and sabotage, but in the end the stoop was accepted. Many viewed it as the beginning of Shank's decline.

By bobbing and leaning like a boxer's second Missy had established through windows that no one of substance was in the bar as yet. Hence her wait. It didn't pay to be first of the evening, as it didn't to be seen alone too often, as though your life were as empty as the chapel lot's bottles. The best you could do barwise to help your image was stroll in at midnight, glance around, bite down a yawn, and leave again. Missy had never dared.

An increase in the clarity of that cheery voice made Missy realise that it did not, after all, belong to Store Marsha. It was from outdoors. It came from along the lane descending to her rear. It belonged to someone approaching.

With the sureness of practice, Missy bent over while lifting a foot to pretend she had stopped to check her shoe, at the same time peering back to see if the act was warranted by the voice-owner being in view. She saw no one, only heard a growing trudge from around the next cabin down.

Light as a leopard Missy went on, across the hardtop and onto Gustav's stoop, where a light gleamed coyly. In pushing the rickety door open she looked away to call out at the night, "Okay, I'll try to make it!" Smiling at how difficult it was, being so popular, she went in.

The standard big room, low with its frown of beams, had a crescent of bar in one corner. The rest was tables and bentwood chairs and all the advertisements which decency forbade the use of on exterior walls.

The half-dozen nobodies plus an early tourist couple eating chili kept their eyes on Missy, she was aware, as she went at a precocious saunter to the bar. The attention was warming, a gift. She played to it by ordering loudly, exchanging earthy banalities with Florence, being as extravagant with her movements as a drama-school failure.

Gustav's owner-operator, Florence, a string of sixty, listless from her fifteen-hour days, gave over the can of beer and slipped its tab into Missy's account, one of a shelved row of pewter pots. "Heard about that Brown guy?" she asked. Her voice was as drab as her features.

Not ready to come off-stage, Missy made an elaboration of arms and head while saying, "What about him?"

Florence nodded herself closer over the bar. "They say he's on the run from justice."

"Bullshit. If he was, he wouldn't be making this big deal out of keeping a low profile." She hated the stranger for getting so much notice.

"Billy-John thinks it's true."

That one being an upper major, Missy left the footlights and said in a normal pitch of voice that you never could tell. She gripped her beer. "I mean, you can't."

"I always say that. Always."

Attacking: "Jim's going to check him out any day now."

"Good," Florence said. "Which Jim is that?"

Missy flinched under one eye. "Braddock. Jim and Elsie. You know."

"Oh sure. Sure."

Missy lifted her beer and dared a wink. "Nice guy."

Nodding drably while admitting that the Braddocks had been here forever, right enough, Florence turned toward a doorway. She left on, "Kitchen calls."

Anyway, Missy thought, eight years. That alone was all you needed to be shimmery here. If on top of that you were a good artist—well. So it was going to be nice with Jim, if everything worked out.

Missy took a sip of beer. Turning as smoothly as a slate-miner's ghost she leaned back on the bar. From persistent experience she could tell without looking that she hadn't lost her audience and that the woman tourist was, of course, livid.

Content, Missy put on a somber expression as she went into a searching gaze at a blank stretch of wall, obviously seeing into a mystic distance, the poetess communing with her muse.

The thought that they seemed to be talking more nowadays made Elsie smile. This drew her face out of its ordinariness and into charm, the way a candle unbleaks a room. Elsewhere, charm was a constant: the casual grace, the medium-long hair of glinty auburn, the sly shifting of breasts on a plump body that was all give, the talkative hands.

Elsie wore dresses to the calf, winter's sweaters to the chin. She liked to put the stems of small flowers in her pierced ears and, Jim sometimes told her in moments of high intimacy, she smelt of moonlight and cornflakes.

It was at such moments that Elsie experienced her only

guilt. She looked forward to it, for the pleasure and the assurance of being at least partially complicated.

Elsie had frequent worries about her placidity. She felt sure it was abnormal. If she didn't already know she was intelligent, more so indeed than Jim, which fact annoyed her in some obscure way, she would have considered herself dense.

Others didn't sing to the birds, dance along the village street, decline to regularly take that fifty-mile trip into town, disenjoy household chores. Others couldn't find excitement in crossword puzzles. Others weren't satisfied with their creative work, not without bouts of lovely agonising. It came as a relief, that guilt.

Elsie was not in love with her husband. She did not adore the man she would have wanted for the father of her children, had children been possible. Never did he appear in her dreams, which told her more than she could tell herself. He had never stirred her profoundly. She loved him not at all yet said she did whenever he asked her. The guilt was well deserved.

Elsie, nonetheless, had a deep fondness for Jim. He owned so many weaknesses that she couldn't help but have. Also they had known each other all their lives. She often felt more like his big sister than a wife and she sometimes suspected grotesquely that this could be the reason she so enjoyed making love with him. Elsie stood as firmly against incest as she did against extra-marital sex. She was, Elsie guessed, just an old-fashioned girl at heart.

And yes, she thought, it was nice that they seemed to be talking more. Like the niceness of knowing that, of the two, Jim had the most artistic talent, which was how it should be.

Watching her fingers be nimble, Elsie went on shelling peas. The bad ones she rejected brusquely but without rancour, like passes from the attractive, the pods she occasionally licked inside for the taste of green. She wouldn't have minded betting that she was the only woman in America shelling peas right now.

When Elsie had finished kitchen work she went into the main room. After going to the fireplace end, scuffing her sneakers for the slap-slap, she strode back down to the table, which she circled twice before halting with a wall six feet ahead.

There, she stood with mind composed and arms in the act of astonishment to view the latest Braddock works, which were propped against the wall base.

Jim's theme was figure, Elsie's flora/landscape, as they always were. Both, like all their recent efforts, were in blue. Color of crayon went by period with the Braddocks. Generally they discovered at about the same time the challenge of green, or brown's acute possibilities. This spring they were nodding over blue to show they had known all along that this was truly it.

Hands framing the way as if they wanted to get together and pray, Elsie concentrated on her own new sketch. She had to admit that she was pleased with it. The whole had a pure touch while at the same time managing to be commercial. That was important. People knew what they liked and they liked what they knew, trees and stuff, rocks.

The Braddocks lived on the sale of their work. Twice a year they had a two-man exhibition in town, the sales fair, the newspaper's warm critique written by a Shankite; summer days found one or the other sitting by a roadside pitch in the village, competing with the open-air shows of painters, carvers, weavers, potters. Marsha had sketches on sale in the store at a 30 percent commission, which she sometimes declined to deduct if it was Elsie who went to collect. Like fat mice, the Braddocks lived in amiable indigence.

Elsie let her hands join. They gave one another a good rub and wrap, responding to their owner's unexpected urge for work. She tutted as though at a demanding child, frowning over tolerant eyes, before giving in, head tilting of a sudden. Jim wouldn't mind going without a cooked dessert.

Swaying like a willow in a sweet breeze Elsie went over to the work breakfront. Its top was a conspiracy of flotsam. She chose a blue crayon, which she began to sharpen. On the third stroke she nicked her finger. As she fed on the blood she gave up thanks with white-flashing eyes that Jim was out. She hated to see him shudder.

Despite them being done mainly to make the doer feel noble, or to baste his reputation, or from his wish to be free of the guilt that could follow failure to do them, acts of charity are sometimes performed out of kindness.

Knowing this, John never felt animosity in respect of an approach, only a flat weight at the repetition of it all—on top of his tinge of fear. Therefore he sighed when the knocking happened; sighed, and kept in his place at the table opposite the door.

Another knock came, beating up to, "Hello there! I'm your neighbour—Jim Braddock."

As quietly as a frail burglar, John laid down his knife and fork. He looked a sad reproach at the door, in need of somewhere to place the blame.

"Hello! Hello, Mr. Brown!"

Still quietly, John got up to go to the front window. Despite possible danger being in the future, not now, he unknowingly went in a suggestion of creep, his head lowered.

John was a mild, hurt-looking man in his early forties. His medium build seemed a reduction, since his jeans and sweater drooped like wind-hungry sails, their cuffs overlong. He had lank brown hair wearing off at the crown.

Only his face gave John a touch of distinction, and that not on account of the regular features themselves but in the way they appeared to be attendant on the ailing, dark-sunk, elusive eyes, like guards or nurses.

Obliquely John peered through the loose-knit drapes and the net curtains across the window. He saw a familiar figure, that Braddock man from along the lane. He seemed to be alone. By his attitude it was clear that he knew someone was home.

He knocked again. "Are you all right in there?"

That was always a problem, John fretted. If they didn't get satisfaction they were liable to take a turn for the dramatic, think of aiding the sick or discovering the dead, so force an entry or go to the authorities.

John moved to the door. Through it he said, "I'm in the middle of lunch."

Braddock: "What? Lunch?"

"I meant supper."

"Are you all right?"

"Perfectly, thank you," John said. He knew he was going to have to open up. "I'm not very sociable, that's all."

Tone offended: "Sorry. I just thought I'd do the neighbourly thing."

"Are you alone?"

"Why, yes."

John drew back two bolts, pulled the door open. "Hello."

"Jim Braddock."

"John Brown." They reached with leans to shake hands,

as if each thought the other might be catching. "Do you want to come in," John said, "for a minute?"

Inside, Jim Braddock strolled to the hearth-facing chesterfield. With a faint smile as though to show that his interest was polite, not nosy, he looked around at the rental barrenness. Briefly, his eyes fumbled at the open suitcase spilling paperbacks.

John said he read a lot. Still looking around, Jim Braddock talked of the various people who had rented the cabin over the past eight years. John said repeatedly, "Is that right?"

Braddock looked at him. "Don't let me interrupt your supper."

"It can wait. I'd offer you a drink but I don't have anything around. I'm not much of a drinker."

"My wife, Elsie, she said I could ask you over to eat with us. But I'm too late."

"Yes." They both nodded at the plate on the table. Braddock said, "Some other time."

"Listen," John said. He held his forearms. "Listen. I might as well tell you I'm antisocial. In the sense that I don't mix. I like people but I'm too busy. That's how it is."

"What is it you keep busy at, John?"

"I meditate a lot. I'm about to start as soon as I've had supper."

"You don't paint or anything? Most of us around here, we're into the arts."

Backing toward the door, John said he was strictly a non-artist; when he wasn't meditating he was studying philosophy or reading fiction, he didn't want to offend anyone but he did prefer being alone. "I never entertain. I never go to people's houses."

"Well, that's fine," Jim Braddock said.

"Please thank your wife for me. It was kind of her."

"We're having meatloaf."

"I'll probably never meet her because that would spoil the chain of my meditation. Women particularly do that. It's tough, but there you are."

Braddock said, "Yes." He came forward as though warily, his eyes taut.

"I'm afraid I'm a bit of a freak," John said. "But harmless." He shrugged, freed his hands, smiled.

"We're pretty crazy here ourselves, John. You'll be right at home in Shank." He stopped nearby.

"But listen. You'd be doing me a favor if you let it be known around about me. You know, that I'm sort of antisocial, that I don't want people coming here."

"Sure," Jim Braddock said. "Nobody's going to bother you, though. They're the reverse in these parts."

John opened the door. He made himself do it because there was no other way. Braddock seemed a nice guy and his wife looked even better (her name was Elsie), but this was as far as it could go, and it would have been safer if it hadn't come as far as this.

Looking at the open door-frame Jim Braddock said he guessed he would be running along now. With that old, familiar soreness of regret, like a chance missed, John thanked him for calling, saw him out, and closed the door. He went back to the table.

His beans and french fries were cold. John didn't mind, was even distantly grateful for the event of a spoiled lunch. Spearing a bean at a time, a fry at a time, he played back the visit scene and worked at getting it verbatim. He debated with traces of heat whether he had used this word or that, he invented the gestures he failed to recall, he dissected Braddock's responses to the lies to see if he had accepted them as truths.

His own manner, John decided, had been just right. The

situation he had made iron-clad clear without being too offensive or too strange, and referring to yourself as a freak always put people on the defensive for you.

Everything was going to be fine, John told himself, pausing over his food to put on a stern face, be convincing. There was not a thing to get paranoid about.

Spearing on, John started to plan what next. He could play a game of cards or Scrabble, read magazines or a historical romance, or listen to the radio. If there was enough light in the sky, he could go up the hill. He could bake bread.

John knew, however, that with his post-meal cigarette he would most likely lie on the couch and begin to pretend. He would be along the lane, having supper with the Braddocks. Creating all the dialogue, he would be witty and entertaining, as well as a good listener. They would have a fun evening.

TWO

Elsie swung down the lane to the skirl of her hum. It was a snappy morning with the promise of sun, and, as if this weren't enough, ahead lay the pleasure of shopping. Soon Elsie's mouth opened to let the hum go free.

Still damp at noon, the dirt lane wound downward between foothill mounds as voluptuous as the hips of a fat horse. The pines stood back, silent in the stillness, waiting for the wind that would give them life.

Just before the last bend, around which lane met hardtop at the village edge, Elsie ended her walk and wordless song to stare into the trees. She was looking for the spot where a sliver of snow had persisted, shrinking as the dying do, turning mottled and grey and ugly.

The snow had gone. As she registered the fact, Elsie concaved her body briefly, like someone avoiding a playful punch to the stomach. She walked on.

Her sadness was mild, unfortunately. She would have preferred something stronger, had expected more of her ploy with the snow that was clinging to life.

But then, of course, this disappointment itself was a bonus, Elsie saw, as was the fact that things rarely turn out the way you want. Also she still had the head-heavy pine that was fighting, nobly and beautifully, to stay up, its lean increasing day by day; and the Milanos' staggering marriage; and Jennifer's battle to beat alcohol.

Hum back behind her lips, Elsie rounded the bend.

Shank opened out to her eyes as though it came a-creeping, the effect heightened by lazy chimney smoke drifting away in the opposite direction.

As well as cabins siding the road and each off-shoot of lane, there were vehicles, though most looked no more capable of mobility than the log structures looked ready to go. The Beetles, campers, and pick-ups were enlivened by an occasional dash of variety: the moneyed interloper's new station-wagon, the sedan of an individualist.

Walking the hardtop between cabins Elsie called out here a greeting, threw back there a wave. She felt like a duchess. How sear it would be, it occurred to her, a regular theme, if she and Jim had to move away from Shank, go live in the real world.

The final few yards to the store Elsie skipped, there being no observers. She entered heartily so that the bell would have itself a real good ring. Marsha called a "Hi" from behind her counter and the nobody customer looked around shyly from her browsing. Elsie set out to talk to the unknown woman, determined not to embarrass herself.

Partly for convenience and the visual effect, part out of inefficiency and sloth, the room was a mayhem of goods, an Aladdin's cave of the mundane. Offerings to eat, wear, or sew, articles of metal, wood, and paper, they got in each other's way like children hoping to be picked. What didn't have space below, dangled from above. Shank's store gave every first-timer a strange shudder of recognition or a stab of sadness for a missed childhood memory.

While listening to the customer talk, apologetically, as if on account of the subject matter's drabness, about her husband's influenza, Elsie was thinking Jim.

He had certainly become more communicative. Last night he had praised the meatloaf at flattering length, had chatted away like anything, and later had said he thought he would wander down to the village for a drink. Something, obviously, was on his mind. It was a something that pleased him. He had that puffiness around his mouth. Could it be he was leaving blue behind?

"That's great," Elsie told the woman on seeing Marsha come out from behind her counter. "Be good." She turned away with a hint of genuflection, rounded a pillar of cereal boxes. "Hi, hon."

"Aren't I the busy li'l bee today?" Store Marsha said after giving Elsie a kiss. "I love it." She was in her early forties and looked half Indian with her dark skin, hooked nose, hair blackest near the shoulder and brown at the parting. She wore a headache band of the same beaded type as the oddments that decorated her floor-duster dress.

Daily doings having been given their run, Marsha said, "You heard what they're saying about that John Brown? I never did go for the name."

"He's a bank robber or something. It's silly. He wouldn't come here where he sticks out like a sore thumb."

Marsha walked two fingers up Elsie's arm. "It's fifty miles to the nearest cop, baby."

"Even so. And all you'd have to do is make a phone call to that cop and you'd soon find out what he was, John Brown."

"And spoil the mystery?"

Elsie raised her chin and made her eyebrows grand. "I invited him to dinner last night."

Marsha played boggle. "You didn't."

Elsie, natural again: "I sent Jim. I said, 'Go ask him to eat with us, for God's sake.' "

"You are something else."

"I mean, it was about time."

"So go on."

"Jim saw him. He got right in there. They talked for ages but he wouldn't come for dinner."

Moving sideways closer Marsha put an arm around Elsie's waist. "I want to hear all of it. I suppose everyone knows already."

Elsie said she hadn't breathed a word, she hadn't seen anybody. "Anyway, there's not much to tell. A bit weird though." She gave a fair version of what Jim had reported, Marsha nodding off and repeating the salients: Lunch. Non-drinker. Meditation. Woman avoider. Recluse.

"It looks," Elsie said, "as though Mr. Brown is nothing more than a nice quiet crank."

Marsha dropped her arm. "Bet you he's got agoraphobia or something. Fear of open spaces." As if offering evidence she told a kettle above, "He paid three months' rent in advance." She looked down: "You know, I saw Jim last night and he didn't mention it, seeing Brown."

"He's preoccupied," Elsie said and at the same moment realised how Marsha must feel, knowing less than others about the stranger. Elsie's want of sensitivity made her weave like a girl about to recite.

She said, "If I was you I'd go up there and ask him if everything's okay. You're the agent, sort of."

Marsha threw out her enjoyable laugh, the one that grabbed your lungs. "The hell with him," she said.

One morning in Dublin, on a post-school drunk in Europe, Jim went into a pub to lose his trembles. Only two customers were bearing the new-washed smell: an old man at the bar, an old woman at a corner table drinking Guinness. On joining the man Jim saw that he was less old by years than by alcohol abuse, his stance a teeter, his face a livid quilt; a man in physical despair.

He asked, "Hear the one about . . . ?" Pity made Jim act a laugh at the yesteryear joke, fear urged him into standing the man a beer. They toasted each other and drank, while the old woman in the corner with a Guinness watched in sad benediction.

Years passed before Jim realised it was because of that brief scene that he had never again let drink get the better of him, use him instead of him using it. Since then, he had never been so drunk that he couldn't see the old woman in the corner with a Guinness.

So in Gustav's, late afternoon, feeling muzzy, Jim made his third drink a Coke. He didn't mind that the two majors with whom he leaned on the bar began to lecture on the evils of sugar, talking over and at one another as if they disagreed. A, they weren't deriding his declination of alcohol, and B, they were standing here with him on equal terms, just as though they hadn't been Shankites for twenty-odd years. He wished there were other people around.

Which seemed to make the door open and admit a newcomer. The contender's beard and peajacket, unlike those of the other pair, had the uncomfortable mien of clothes on a circus dog.

Jerking a thumb behind he said, "That Missy, she has more trouble with her shoes than anyone I ever knew."

What this meant Jim didn't bother to consider, registering simply that Missy was at hand, on her way. While the other two ignored the man, went on agreeing belligerently about sugar, Jim gave him a faint smile and a tilt of the head, wanting to be on the safe side. Last fall a contender had become a near-major by walking all the way to town while playing a violin.

However: as the newcomer reacted to recognition, came toward the bar, Jim randomly moved out from it to circle away, around to his companions' other side. In doing so he told them, with a coarseness that spoke of familiarity, "You guys slay me."

New position settled, Jim mused that she was coming. What had appeared to be, was: they would meet this afternoon, same place. He hadn't been sure. During last night's hour of talk in bursts, snatches passed over or behind other customers like stolen property (they had avoided standing together), that date at dusk had been as uncertain as the meaning in Missy's eye-language, though the play of her bottom lip was more implicit. And when she had paused behind him in leaving, to walk home with neighbour Rachel, the nuisance, she had slid the edge of her hand neatly between his buttocks. That would seem to be significant.

Jim waited. He sipped his Coke, felt a devil, kept a glancing watch on the door. Murkiness came closer to the window.

Missy arrived, pushing inside with a wave to someone in the distance. Jim took satisfied note of that in addition to the way she didn't deign to greet the major pair as she came to the bar at a stroll.

The contender said a heavily casual, "Hi there, Missy." They always used names.

Missy nodded. It was an automatic response. She was mentally busy, appreciating Jim's airy lean as well as the company he was keeping, while in respect of said company praying for the best.

Standing at the bar, eyes down like a nun on a train, Missy hoped they would say nothing to hurt her. Not Jim, the pair between. Jim, he was on, that seemed sure after last night's business of eyes and mouth, to which she believed she had responded in acceptable style.

Missy was pleased with how the burgeoning affair was

doing. She might even have confided in Rachel except for suspecting that Rachel fancied Jim herself.

Still feeling his two bourbons Jim looked along in front of the majors, who were maligning caffeine. He eased one foot tautly off the floor to say a bright, "What'll you have, on me?"

Missy looked around. "Oh, hi there. Gee thanks. I'll have what you're having."

"Me, I'm coasting on a Coke."

Telling Jim she would have the same, Missy told herself that his choice alone showed just how he stood in Shank. You had to be inner than Flynn to get away with drinking pop around here.

Florence came out like a speedy snail. After serving Missy she kept her talking until there were new arrivals. The three nobodies skimmed their semi-lowered gazes past everyone except the contender, whom they greeted, "Hi, Harry." He gave three nods. The majors left and Missy sidled closer to Jim in copy of his own sidling. With the same dirge of enthusiasm as had brought her out, Florence went back to the kitchen.

"I heard," Missy said, "that your John Brown's a moonshiner."

"That's a new one."

"He's got a whole damn still in there, I heard."

Jim blew out his lips in a negative. "There's nothing in the place that wasn't there before. Hardly."

"You peeked in?"

"I dropped by to see him last night."

"Just like that?" Missy asked, not hiding how impressed she was due to feeling irked. It was like being helped out in an emergency by someone you loathed.

Jim said he hadn't stayed all that long. "An hour or so."

"No still?"

"Not a one."

Missy sipped, put down her drink. "Talking of 'shine," she said. "I scored a great bottle recently. Would you care for a little shot?"

"What a brilliant idea," Jim said because it was expected, speaking in veiled pomposity because of feeling rebuffed over his John Brown news. "Sure." He hated moonshine.

"If you really want to," Missy said.

Their eyes played tease, each pair circling the other, skipping to and from, never quite meeting. Missy said, "When I leave, why don't you follow me down after about ten minutes?"

Urban dandruff began to appear, his headlight picking out cans, bottles, and condoms on the road's shoulder. The unlovely was joined by the vicious: bullet-bent signs. Next came the billboards with their glib pledges or threats or pleas.

Minding the one about loved children, John reduced the speed of his motor cycle. Not that he had been going fast. He never did, though this was connected only on a slant to the adage that speed killed. What speed couldn't kill was the time available when the goal was made.

John steered at a chug into the parking-lot, where cars were tailing each other out like grumbling convicts. He circled, came to a sidewalk, drew to an unplanned stop in the blast of light from a drugstore.

It was worthwhile. He felt vulnerable, afraid, faintly thrilled, almost special. Smiling for confidence like a liar on trial he raised both hands to settle, be aware of, his crash-helmet.

The surface of the store window showed John himself in the style of a simplified astronaut, his zip-up unbulky due to the cool nudity beneath, his features a mere suggestion behind the globe's front of smoked plastic. A common enough figure nowadays and not without appeal, John allowed himself to think.

It was one of the smaller cabins on the settlement's lower reaches, where once upon a less happy time had lived the blacks, at liberty to look down on one another for density of color or proximity to slavery. Rachel embarrassed everybody by calling the section Niggertown.

Like an ugly gnome in search of a melting wish, Missy darted around the room in a stoop. She was changing its character. She flung cushions onto the bed to make it into a divan, jiggled skimpy curtains across to hide the kitchen equipment, did a general untidying to give the place that insouciant, Bohemian look. Movie magazines were hidden, an Auden and a Plath brought to unaccustomed light.

With a forefinger pushing up her nose piggily, Missy stood and gazed about. It would do, she thought. Be better if she had a joss-stick going and if it were after midnight, but it would do.

In a final dart Missy went to the window, where she drew weighty drapes and killed the twilight. The improvement she nodded at while avoiding thoughts of seduction being easier in gloom. Suddenly she wished she were drunk, or in hell. She cupped her brow and chin for reassurance.

Trouble was, Missy acknowledged, she didn't have much of a yen for Jim Braddock. He was nice, she liked him, but he didn't make anything happen inside her the way some men did.

Missy told herself you couldn't have everything. The real sexy majors were unavailable. It was Jim or no one.

Uplifted by the reminder that his wife was attractive and nice, flattering, Missy hurried into the bathroom.

Missy was naked under a robe and had sprinkled water on her head by the time she heard the front door open to a call of "Hello there." She counted to five before looking through the bathroom's part-open door.

With the front door ajar Jim was leaning his head and shoulders inside. "Oh, there you are," he said.

Missy said, "It's you."

"Yes."

"I was just stepping into the shower."

Jim felt despondent. "You were?"

"I thought you'd changed your mind. About the drink."

Cheering up grimly: "It wasn't a drink I was really interested in."

Missy told herself that here they went, it was on. She said a shy-sounding, "I didn't think you were, somehow."

"Maybe I'm just making a social call."

"That's always possible."

"I'll come in," Jim said, entering with a glance back to check the continuing all-clear. "I'll bolt the door." He wished to Christ he'd had another bourbon.

To remove any doubt as to the illicit nature of his presence Missy asked, "Did anyone see you come?"

"No. I was careful."

"If they did, it might get mentioned."

He moved across the room. "Know what you mean."

As Missy moved through the doorway and into a slow, neat, effortless embrace with Jim her mind was mainly on the curious fact that she couldn't recall ever having made love when straight. That, she heeded, was why she felt jittery, as well as from the Coke. It had nothing to do with not fancying Jim.

With the comfort of a woman's body in his arms, Jim

took another rung up from his despondency. He felt the warmth of achievement and the hauteur of power; felt near to being in control of the situation. Closing his eyes to prove this to himself he snuggled against the soft cheek and roved his hands over the silk-coated back as if he meant it.

Having a woman in his arms was all very well, drifted Jim's mind, but they couldn't go on standing here forever. When he had tried to peck around to the front for a kiss, she had stayed clamped.

Missy backed off. "I'm going to light a candle. Can I watch you get undressed?"

At gratifying long last in his suburban prowl John had found a suitable store. It was open for business, it was small, it was quiet. Two women in housecoats padded among the shelved groceries, another in a smock guarded the single check-out.

John went in. Acting the haste which would go toward explaining why he didn't remove his helmet, should its presence be found strange here, he snapped up a basket and went along an aisle. His list of needs he had mentally perfected hours ago. He filled it in snatches and pounces, meanwhile whistling to show how light was his state of mind, how harmless his haste. Every detail helped.

After initial looks of surprise, both shoppers gave up on John as an object of interest as completely as though he had tried to sell them a prayer. Similar was the cashier's response, although she closed the matter with a smile to express a kind of understanding. This, bringing softness to a face which complained of hardship, made John sorry he couldn't tell her to be thankful for meagre mercies.

He left the store with his usual looseness of relief at having once again come safely through the peril of shopping. Ten minutes later John was on Main, going into a picture show with two hot dogs and a box of popcorn. The movie he had seen last year, but the other two showing in town he had seen more recently than that.

Despite having drawn a glare from the box-office girl and from the usher a frown of warning, John had yet to remove his helmet. He did so once seated in darkness among a dozen patrons who were spread like stars on a dull night, as if they wanted to deny any suggestion of an unwanted solitude. The hot dogs and popcorn were made to last through many reels.

Implacable as rain-forest damp, John sat the show around to his point of entry. Helmet he put on while walking up the aisle. Outside he went to Main Street's dwindling end, to the bar he had looked in at last week, where the television was low and the all-male crowd docile.

Nothing had changed, John saw on going in: twenty-odd men at the counter and tables, white collars outnumbering blue, ambience as casual as just plain folks. The provincial's desire to be thought sophisticated kept attention from resting too long on the odd-clad newcomer.

John took a stool at the bar. He waited, scanning around openly, until the barman came before lifting off his crash-helmet with a sigh that would seem to call for comment. The barman, young and flabby, manner cruel as a croupier's in its disinterest, asked, "And yours?"

That John ordered beer was less out of preference than the drink could be made to last longer. During the serving-paying he tried to get the barman into conversation, scooting back a quarter tip and, as if he were one of those travellers with a thousand magical tales to tell, asking about good hotels in these parts.

"Plenty up Main," the man said.

Maybe next time, John thought. He settled to a forward hunch and a gaze at bottles. He knew every bottle in the house. He had seen them all before in a hundred similar places, just as he had been through this manoeuvre a hundred times. He knew there might be nothing other than bottles ahead for company this evening, that the barman could stay aloof and the other solo customers hold their solo status intact.

John sat on in his hunch while wearing a light smile. He sipped beer like a miser, watched bottles, toyed with his cigarettes and matches without lighting up; tried not to catch the barman's eye too often, gave the bottles a count, noted via their backing mirror the situation with other loners along the bar; glanced at the television, sat up in preparation as a man came alongside and sagged again when he left after buying a cigar; finished off his warming beer, lit a cigarette for the gift of it, and started looking for the bottle label with the right letters to make the word *death*.

"That's a fine helmet you got there."

The speaker was middle-aged, suavely dressed, respectable to his tie's shapely knot, face inclined to be dingy as though he sat in a back room in a job that gave him no power.

John dropped a hand atop his helmet, the action one almost of affection. This wasn't the first time the globe had been a help. "Thanks," he said.

"Yes sir. Real fine."

John flattered, suggesting youth, with, "You're a biker?"

"Hell no. The automobile's good enough for me."

"Certainly safer."

The man said he had only ever been on a motor cycle once in his whole entire life and that was when he was ten years old. "I can remember it like yesterday."

Smiling: "That right?"

It was an amusing story. The man told it while getting a whisky, exchanging names, accepting a cigarette even though he was a Camel man himself and supplying lights with a lighter which he said was gold. He said it twice.

John ordered a beer. He encouraged Harry to talk so it would be only fair if presently he had a turn at talking, which, he knew, it would be difficult to stop himself from doing. He would talk about anything, lie, but stay off the topics he knew most thoroughly: love and loneliness.

It was slowly that John realised the sense being made by Harry's eyes, his gestures, and the occasional word. They were stating, informing, that he was a homosexual. Inevitably, the statement was towing a question.

Inside him, John faded like a dying spark. He felt bitter and stale and more alone than ever. Moreover there was the awkwardness of a situation which hadn't occurred often enough for him to have created a standard gambit, an out that didn't cause hurt. It was so easy to hurt. There had been too much of that and he had never wanted to hurt anyone.

As sometimes happened, triggered by a sight, a thought, a murmur, the enormity of his life presented itself to John's consciousness with a sudden flush, like crashing open shutters to the sun. His stomach clenched, his breath held. He shot up a hand to contain the trembling of his lips.

"Say, Bill," Harry said in grinned alarm, "you're not going to throw up, are you?"

Weaving his head as a type of nod, John scooped his helmet off the bar and quitted the stool. He strode to the door, went out, hurried along the street.

THREE

With the surrounding foliage being permanently green, spring approached as gently as the growth of jowls, as unseen in consensus as Shank's quiet decay. Life in the village took its usual ambling course. Enjoyable crises, causing people to gather: the store running out of milk, a battered-wife situation, a sculptor running amok because his rent had been doubled. Mystery newcomer Brown continued to show no interest in the established locals, forcing them to lose public interest in the man, so that only nobodies mentioned his name, inadvertently.

Jim pursued his social aims. He went again to Missy's place, at night, after he and she had spent an intriguing two hours at a drab party, sitting apart and hardly looking at each other at all. His main concern now over the relationship was how long it would take for word of it to get solidly around.

Having been told by Elsie that white men were intimidated by, and generally acquiesced to, black women, Store Marsha took Rachel with her when she went to see John Brown. He apologised through the door for not opening up. Influenza, he said.

Missy was delighted with herself. Frequently she patted her chest. Knowing that married men were often as mechanical as rabbits, bed bores, she forgave Jim for his uninspired lovemaking while determining to bring him along gradually.

Elsie felt a slight discomfort, like owing a favour. Jim hadn't made love to her lately and she was missing her guilt. Several times she told him how much better an artist he was than she, which helped, the protestation giving her the impression that she was lying. Having a lovely time feeling neurotic, a mess, she smiled at herself.

Min Kuzak came out to spend the night in her cabin. After a coffee with Elsie she went to make a formal call on her new neighbour. He declined to open the door. The reasons he gave included the inability of his eyes to stand light. To Elsie, Min Kuzak said, "Screw 'im."

To everyone to whom she occasionally wrote, Missy wrote, pouring out her sorrow at being involved with this man who belonged to another, a man whose name she couldn't give because he was pretty famous in the art world.

John opened his door to Jim Braddock repeatedly, with lessening reluctance. Braddock came to borrow-return books. In his company John felt an increasing ease, prompting him to wonder, was it possible to have a friend?

One of the larger cabins would make an ideal restaurant, Early American in theme, said a tourist. People would be happy to drive from miles around to experience the real, genuine thing, he said, thoughtful. Local laughter turned nervous when it became known that the tourist owned a chain of restaurants in Alabama.

After the third session with Jim, Missy stopped wrong-buttoning her blouses. This she emphasised by affixing at the top a large safety-pin, which, when among people, she fiddled with constantly, as though it were a new-gifted brooch. No one mentioned the change.

Since Jim hadn't touched a crayon in days, was given to mooning when he wasn't talking to her like a gossip (which was nice, no knock), Elsie decided that consciously or otherwise he was heading for a new direction in his art. Feeling remiss, having no desire to change her style or medium, she sang more than usual when about her chores.

A major who had notions of buying a motor cycle went to John Brown's cabin. Exchange conducted through the keyhole, he said he had seen him with his machine on the highway and would be prepared to give a fair price. Curtly John Brown told him he had no intentions of selling.

Jim liked calling in on his neighbour. On his fifth or sixth visit they had a game of Scrabble. Although the host started out brilliantly he fell apart toward the end, losing by many points. It was quality that told in the long run, Jim guessed.

It came to Missy that what she had written to friends about Jim's fame, which she wholeheartedly believed, could someday be true. There was, sure, a good chance of him becoming a celebrated artist. She could be up there with him. And if not, she could be renowned as his former mistress, the woman who had been a great influence on his art, like Gertrude Stein and Scott Fitzgerald. Missy was impressed, even though this was somehow expected, she always having felt she was a little on the special side. She strengthened the hints she had been ekeing about the relationship.

On their second game of Scrabble, two days after the first, John again let Jim Braddock win, which was entertainingly difficult to bring about. That Jim was nervously pleased was evidenced by the fact that, in talking afterwards about his marriage (a good one, it seemed), he repeatedly called his wife by another name.

Sunday afternoon, after Jim had gone out to take a walk, Elsie got herself ready to join Marsha for tea. Showered and changed, hair worked on to give it that ignored look, she put the stems of daisies through the holes in her earlobes and told her reflection it was sensational. She set off from home like a star leaving her dressing room.

Around behind the cabin Elsie went to a point rearward of the Kuzak place, where the ground took a sudden drop. Going down onto a flight of rough-hewn steps, arms wary, she began on the short-cut to the village. She hummed.

It didn't matter that when last seen her tree was holding on rapaciously, or that the Milanos seemed to have hit a calm patch, Elsie felt nice and complex. After all, it wasn't every woman whose husband might possibly be going through an artistic crisis.

The series of steps and slopes ended near the chapel lot. Another minute and Elsie was sauntering toward Gustav's, where Marsha waited with the stoop to herself. Their waves made and then caricatured, as if greetings were infantile or should be joshed for lacking the weight of farewells, she went inside to get the tea.

Arriving, sitting, Elsie was reminded of a recent addition to her fret-list. For the first time in seventeen years, word had it, Penelope Parsons would not be coming to Shank for her usual summer break from television work.

The precise nature of her discontent at the news was muddy to Elsie. What would she miss—Pen's impromptu skits on the midnight stoop, or being able to claim one of the medium-famous as a bosom pal?

Or, Elsie wondered with a blink, was it simply that nowadays you never heard anything positive in connection with Shank?

Marsha came out with a tray. Already on the table were the home-made brownies she had brought herself. After a kiss and a compliment the partaking began, and after her acting ability had been derided by Marsha the subject of Penelope Parsons was dropped.

"What's wrong with your shirt?" Elsie asked. "Or has the store run out of buttons?"

Touching the large safety-pin Marsha said it was the latest accessory fashion, somebody must have brought it from town or Atlanta. "Every other lady around here's wearing one."

Elsie said it went to show they weren't so out of touch as people might think. "Right?"

"Right, baby."

"Scrumptious brownies."

Marsha patted her knee. "Made 'em just for you."

Recipes mixed with the thin come and go of patrons occupied them until Marsha asked mildly, "Isn't that Jim?"

It was, Elsie saw when she finally looked around from pouring herself a second cup and putting down the teapot. Ambling along, her husband was coming up the lane across the way. As if the ground were being witty, he wore a faint smile.

"A million miles away," Marsha said.

Instead of trying to explain about creative crises, which Marsha, a non-artist, might not understand, Elsie said lightly, "He's probably been seeing a woman."

"What makes you say that, baby?"

"Nothing. Only it's a funny way for him to go walking, down there." She hadn't known she was going to voice what she wasn't fully sure she had been thinking.

"Well, listen," Marsha said. "I'll tell you something."

Jim, arrived at the store corner, saw the two women while making a turn onto the hardtop. As though struck by a vast truth, he came to a jangly halt, his arms loose. He looked across steadily, nodding like an unenthusiastic doubter, smile on at a flicker.

Elsie raised a salute of "Hello." Jim, straightening, signalled the same and that he would continue his walk. He went on at a stride.

Elsie turned to Marsha. "We were saying?"

"I wasn't going to tell you. Christ, it's nothing. But anyway."

"Anyway."

"Here in the bar a while back," Marsha said as comfortably as a once-upon-a-time, "Rachel was seen feeling Jim's ass."

"Well now," Elsie said placidly.

"She was standing behind him, talking to someone, and giving Jim's ass a good feel."

"So you never know."

"Rachel always did have a little yen for Jim."

"And she lives down there," Elsie finished. "Sure, you never know." She was quietly thrilled. She felt worldly. The part she had been given to play, maybe, that of cheated wife, she liked, for she had nothing to worry about, knowing that Jim's love for her was absolute.

A romantic intrigue (the reason for all that mooning?) could do the world of good for Jim, Elsie thought. She was liberally glad it might be Rachel, who was always cheery, was a year older than Jim, and had no calves to speak of.

Elsie did admit to herself that perhaps she preferred to believe in an affair than in the chance of being left behind artistically. That gave her a thrill as well.

In social intercourse the need for a confidant is stronger than the greed for success, since success, if no one knows about it, is only lack of failure.

Although Jim didn't realise how greatly he felt in want

of a close friend, an ear, in Shank or elsewhere, he did know that if he didn't soon tell someone about Missy he would be apt to blurt it out in the wrong place.

Which, Jim knew, would never do. He hated to come on like a rube. Time would take care of the pseudo-secret circulation (there was no real hurry) and if anyone then were crude enough to ask him if he was giving it to Missy he would put on a fine act of denial, stylishly protest too much.

Meanwhile, Jim had to tell privately. He had to beat his chest.

That John Brown formed the perfect ear didn't occur to Jim until after he had nearly told Elsie. This evening, catching her looking at him with one of her long gazes, he twitched to the threshold of a telling. After all, he defended as heat prickled his armpits, there was no one closer to him on earth than his wife.

She asked, gaze flicked off, "Something wrong?"

"Thought I heard something outside."

"Wind. It's a windy, black night. Very black."

"Maybe it was John's bike."

Elsie shook her hair, making glints. "Went by an hour ago, about. Didn't you say this was the night he was going to town for groceries?"

"I guess," Jim said.

"Not much good to our local economy, your Mr. Brown."

"Did you wave to him?"

"I was outside getting a log. Sure. He gave me the usual bow. It must be suffocating in that stupid helmet. Just wait till summer comes."

John was perfect, Jim thought, on the heels of which he agreed that it wouldn't be in the shape of a telling. He, the younger man, would be asking the older for advice. There was this difficult situation. An emergency, you could say.

With shoulder shuffles of enthusiasm Jim scooped at his macaroni. Lenient, he answered as well he could Elsie's questions about what he had seen of interest on his walk today. There was no sense in telling of the one memorable point (Missy had been out, posing somewhere), which came because he had the days confused. He was startled to see Elsie and Marsha on the bar stoop, having just been thinking that if this were Sunday instead of Saturday, there they would be. And there they were. It had been like seeing ghosts.

Two hours later Jim heard the motor cycle rumble past. He closed his historical romance. "That's John. I'm going to take this book back."

Nodding over her crossword puzzle magazine, Elsie said, "Watch your step. It's a black night out there."

Jim left. Along the lane he went noisily, warningly, around to the end cabin's rear, where John was manhandling his machine through the kitchen doorway, which sent out a theatrical flood of light. Jim was pleased at that. It gave him a feeling of Christmas. He recognised that he hadn't been so up and coming in years.

Saddle-boxes unpacked, book exchanged, Jim said while easing his feet off the floor, "Actually, John, I came over to talk to you about something." As usual, he was sitting in a corner of the chesterfield to hide a dark stain, which grated on him.

John rose from blowing on the fire. "Is that right?" He turned this way and patted his buttocks as though to assure them they would soon get warm. "That's fine, Jim."

"I promise not to bore you."

"I'm not easily bored."

From his shirt pocket Jim brought out the joint. "This is

very decent stuff. Present from the person in question, as it happens. You do smoke, right?"

"Not much any more. It'll be a nice change."

Jim lit up. After three drags he passed the hashish cigarette up to John, who said, "I won't feel like Scrabble after this."

"Christ no. I didn't come for Scrabble. I wouldn't say no to a beer, though."

When the joint had gone back, and forth, and back, and been killed, John fetched two cans. His eyes like dawn from the narcotic, he leaned on the mantel to sip. He said, "It's only natural that you're curious."

"What?"

"And I wouldn't blame anyone for not believing."

Jim didn't know what he meant. This was often the case when he smoked with others, even with Elsie. Whereas everything he said himself was sharp and to the point, be it serious or one of those hilarious chain-gags he sometimes got on, all perfectly understandable, other people at times talked nonsense. Or they seemed to.

Jim told himself not to go and spoil his high. He was always doing that, worrying if people were being profound and he wasn't getting it.

"I wouldn't want any of it to get around," John said. "If I told you."

"Of course not."

"In fact, if I ask you to give me your word that you won't mention it to anyone, will you?"

"I will," Jim said, feeling fine, knowledgeable, kind. "I'd like the same from you. Nobody knows, you see." He smiled in forgiveness when John took no notice, going on:

"I shouldn't really. But sometimes you have to. You can't help yourself."

"That's it exactly."

"I think I can trust you, Jim."

"We trust each other, John. We really do."

John stood erect from his lean on the mantel. Solemn as an old book he said, "I'm going to tell you. You won't believe me but never mind. If I were in your shoes I wouldn't either. That is quite certain."

After hesitating, Jim decided not to laugh, John looked too radically in earnest for this to be fun. He looked more so as the seconds passed. They passed slowly.

Jim fidgeted, glanced away, sipped his beer, wondering if the host had forgotten what he was going to say, not an uncommon thing. He was about to speak himself when John at last began to talk.

Wearing the light smile of polite interest, like a saint in hell, Jim leaned forward. He noted that whereas John was normally quiescent physically, now he was letting his body help him speak: he swayed, rocked, shaped with his hands, tapped himself gently, sagged at the knees.

Jim also noted, gradually, losing his smile and seeping back into the couch corner, that John's earnestness had given way to another expression. He looked stricken. He looked desperate.

What Jim was less sure of was matter. It came to his hearing as a confused blend of present and past tenses, for one thing. For another, Jim didn't know if the central figure referred to was John himself or another real person or a character in a film, book, play, what had you.

"Oh, I know I'm telling it all backwards," John said, tone bitter. "But you do see, don't you?"

"I think so."

He did, more or less, despite the jumbled story beginning to take on elements of the incredible. He certainly saw that John Brown was telling it with what appeared to be painful sincerity, perhaps even with anguish.

"You understand?" John asked.

Jim nodded. "Yes. Eleven suicides."

"You don't have to believe me."

"That's okay."

"So long as you're listening," John said haggardly.

"I'm listening all right."

"It's something for me to be able to tell it. You have no idea. Thank you."

"That's fine," Jim said.

John said, "They hurt me more than anything." He drooped on the sentence as though it were a saga's closing line. "More than the murders."

"I see."

"There were four murders and four attempts. But those suicides." He stood in a long-armed sag like a hanged ape, reddened eyes fixed in a gape on Jim, who was pressing hard into the corner because he had the terrible suspicion that John Brown was about to weep.

He said, "Well, never mind."

"Two of them were only children," John said, his voice faint and with a hint of squeal, which matched his asthmatic's hunch. "Thirteen years old, fourteen years old. Children." His giving of the last word continued, to become an understated sobbing, one on which he closed his eyes as though in a torment of joy.

"I'm in bed," Elsie called when she heard the front door open. She put her book down as she sat up, at the same time flushing her mind free of spies in the night and blinking to clear her vision of words. She wanted to see if she could tell by looking at her husband if he had been with Rachel.

The black woman went from Elsie's consideration as Jim appeared in the bedroom doorway, even before he let himself slope into a lean against the frame like someone who had just finished doing a chore under duress.

He said, "Well, shit."

"Whatever that may mean."

"You wait."

"How much've you had to drink, hon?"

"One lousy beer. Which I didn't finish. Had a smoke, though. John had this joint."

"How nice," Elsie said with show-envy, despite knowing that a smoke now would keep her from sleeping. "Lucky old you."

"I don't know about that," Jim said. "It's nearly faded anyway. But Christ." He looked to be torn between bewilderment and embarrassment while trying to appear wise and calm.

"What's up?"

"Listen. What an experience. I'm pretty shaken, if you want to know the truth."

Elsie hugged her knees. "Yes, hon, you look it. Did you guys have a fight or something?"

"No no no no," Jim said. "I had nothing to do with it. But maybe there's something about me that makes people cry." He gave a quick shake of his head, hurried on into, "That's what happened with John in the end. He stood there crying, for God's sake."

"John Brown?"

"John Brown, Els. Crying like a kid. I didn't know how to get out."

Elsie nodded encouragement. "What was he crying about?"

Jim said a steady, "Listen. I like the guy. But he's a crazy. He's obsessed. Either that or he was stoned out of his mind. Know what he told me?"

"No, Jim, I do not know what he told you."

"You'll think I'm kidding."

Warningly, Elsie said, "Jim."

"Okay," he said, standing straight and holding out his hands as if to prove they had been washed. "This is the basic. John Brown claims that every woman he meets falls in love with him."

Knowing he was serious, Elsie looked at her husband with a firm gaze. "Well," she said. "That is something."

"You got it?"

"Of course."

Jim came forward, sat on the bed edge. "Every woman who sees John more than once falls in love with him, according to John. And desperately. Finally. I never heard the like of that before, did you?"

"He was stoned."

"Somehow, now, I don't think it was that. I think he really believes what he told me."

"That every woman he meets falls for him? Come on. He couldn't believe that."

Jim raised a finger. "Every female, John said, of the child-bearing years. Between about twelve years old and about forty-five, with one exception."

Elsie said it sounded to her like one of those dumb, macho daydreams that grown-up men went in for.

"It does, Els, until you realise it wouldn't be any prize. Right the reverse. More a nightmare than a daydream. Your life wouldn't be your own. You'd be hounded by unhappy women. A goddamn nightmare."

"Is that why he was crying?" Elsie asked, wanting to smile yet finding no facial cooperation.

"That and the rest," Jim said. "He was hurting. And he was serious. He didn't just come out with it. First he made me swear not to tell anyone."

"You're telling me."

"You're my wife, aren't you?"

"Ah well," Elsie said. She shook her head at his frailty while experiencing gratitude for its existence.

Jim said, "His name's not John Brown, as I'd figured. The John's real, the Brown's not. He's had to change it many times and move around a lot. He's used all kinds of tricks to hide his face and stay out of sight."

"It's a wild one all right."

"He daren't let any woman see him more than once, he says. The first time's okay, the second time they fall. He's been fine now for about three months."

Elsie asked, "You mean this fatal attraction deal's been going on for years?"

"For three years he's been living with tragedy, is the way John puts it."

"He called it that—tragedy?"

"It would be," Jim said on a nod. "But that's where it gets kinda sick. If it wasn't for that it'd be a gas, his story."

"Tell me the worst."

"Listen. He says four of the women who fell for him were murdered. By their husbands. Jealousy."

"He really said that?"

"Yes. And another four were wounded."

"Oh come on, John Brown."

"Wait," Jim said, "There's more." He looked less shaken now. "The thing is, women fall head over heels. Violently and passionately. It's not a quiet thing with most of the young ones, as it can be if they're older. It's a great big emotional explosion for them. This is the man they've been looking for and maybe even sort of expecting. They're ready to follow him to the ends of the earth."

"I get the picture, Jim."

"You think I'm exaggerating."

"No, I don't. Honest."

With obvious enjoyment Jim said, "Eleven of the women have committed suicide."

"Yes, that's sick."

"Two were young teenagers."

"Real sick," Elsie said. "Why did he have to go and spoil the story?"

Jim said that was why he thought John believed it. "See, it's not a glamorous story at all. It's not romantic and it's not poignant. It's only weird."

Elsie put her arms under the covers. "Weird and sick."

There was a pause. They nodded at each other. Elsie said, "Next time you go, he might not even mention this."

"Talking of mentioning it," Jim said.

Their discussion on that ended with the agreement not to tell anyone about John Brown's story. People could think them crazy themselves, for evidently John wouldn't be prepared to verify it. Also, Jim pointed out, if the story spread it was bound to get to John, who would know that the spreading could have happened only through his neighbour.

Elsie said she didn't like stories like that anyway. "He should've left the deaths out."

"Another thing," Jim said, getting up and turning toward the doorway. "Half the women in Shank'd be coming up here, giving the poor guy a hard time."

"I wouldn't."

"I mean, it's a harmless enough obsession. He's not hurting anybody, except in his imagination."

After shaking her head thoroughly to show herself she was serious, Elsie said, "From here on I'm not even going to peek at him as he goes by."

Jim, muttering about a sandwich, had gone out. Reappearing in the doorway he asked, "What's that?"

Elsie told him, "I'm superstitious. You are too but you won't admit it. I'm not about to take any risks."

"You have to be kidding, Els."

"If Henry James could believe in strange things, so can I. Not that I think for one single moment that John's stupid, sick story has an ounce of truth in it. But believe me, I'm not taking any chances."

Jim left again on a sighed, "Jesus."

Twenty years ago, in Shank's golden age, poetry readings were always held at noon so as to be different from San Francisco and New York. The practice died without withering during a period when the locals were heavily into anti-pretension. Recently, those optimistic about Shank's future had brought midday gatherings back into fashion.

Missy thought all traditions cute, especially if they meant you got something for nothing. Even if she had not, she still would have welcomed hearing of the reading to be held at Jennifer's place.

After giving in her name as a reader, Missy, stimulated, spent many hours composing a pair of love poems, culling from Robert Graves, Elizabeth Barrett Browning, two radio commercials, and a Gershwin lyric. One poem was from a man to a woman, the other the reverse of that. Although no names were used there would be no doubt in any listener's mind, Missy knew, that the people involved were herself and Jim Braddock.

The fact of plagiarism didn't occur to Missy. Her sole and soon-forgotten qualm came from a suspicion that poetry should be truthful, and here she had not only sacrificed truth for euphony and rhyme, in common with many poets of sterner talents, but had lied outright about the hero. She had stated that he was a master in the art of lovemaking.

Missy thought of that now as she walked with Rachel along the lane toward Jennifer's. The reminder was her poetry crackling in her pocket. She wondered if she ought to get Jim one of those how-to books, if there were any around she could borrow.

She asked, "I don't suppose you'd have a sex manual on your shelves, would you?"

"Sure, making out with a dictionary," Rachel said. "Next it'll be a Bible."

Tutting, Missy flapped a corner of her fringed shawl. "You're a shocker."

"The answer's no, I don't have. Why?"

"Ah," Missy said mysteriously in a bid for passing power, which failed; following a shrug, Rachel began to talk about one of today's poet-readers.

Rachel had the height and slimness of an athlete. She seemed to be all teeth and Afro.

At the cabin door she asked over her shoulder, "That was nice dope I gave you, huh?"

"Great," Missy lied. "Thanks again." The cigarette she had made from Rachel's nub of hashish she had given to Jim. One gift deserves another, had been her motive. So far, the ploy had earned no return, no object of which she could say, "Oh, Jim gave me that."

The living room held some thirty people, most sitting on the floor. Being ignored in her suggestions for seating arrangements was Jennifer, who smiled through her desperate sobriety. May and Jake Milano sat near the dais—a table turned upside-down on squat piles of books. Many of the women wore safety-pins, which went unseen by Missy, as, in common with most females, she took conscious note of fashion only when it was absent, thus pleasurable. She was unaware of the safety-pin craze having developed from self beginnings because she knew her place.

While Rachel went to greet the Milanos, Missy moved to the wall, where she would stand, there being too many sitting on the floor for that to cause interest. Of the Braddocks' absence Missy was gratefully aware. It was tough enough already.

She had her nerve, Missy allowed. This was a pretty brave thing she had planned, making a public declaration through her poetry. She could picture the result. People would start to swap looks and pull their mouths into odd shapes.

Ten minutes passed before Jennifer could bring a semblance of quiet to the group. First poet introduced, and reading, she moved up the room stepping around people and hissing for silence. At Missy's side, after telling her she was on next but one, following May Milano, she went on to malign people for their bad manners in talking while someone was reading.

On the upended table, paper in hand, May said, "Now that we've all settled down and my husband has stopped looking up Rachel's skirt . . ."

While everyone, Rachel included, laughed indulgently, Jake snapped retorts, unheard but seen as salvoes of spittle. Laughter dying uneasily, the matter became clear as references to his wife's intelligence, eyesight, and purity of thought. May told him harshly to shut the hell up so she could read. Jake asked her where, in the first place, she had ever got the idea that she could write poetry.

May Milano's face smoothed to quietly determined. Neatly she said, "Here endeth the first lesson in how to fail at marriage." Stepping down from the table she made aloofly for the door amid a silence which stated that everyone knew the true end had come.

Missy had that force-feed sensation of disappointment. Now, nobody would listen to a word the readers said.

Confession is bad for the soul, since it tempts you to err again in order to get again that lovely simmer from being disdained, as well as to warm-suffer your envy: the confession's recipient is basking in the bonfire glow of his superiority.

This John had known from his religion-colored youth, the smug priests, the struggles of invention to come up with a different sin, which then had to be performed so as to avoid the sin of lying.

What John had not known until recently was that divulgence could have an effect beyond the moments of truth, a following of ease.

Or at any rate, John supposed, this was why he now, walking through the trees, found the birdsong pleasant instead of it being a mockery for his sensibilities. He was altogether less drear of mind, as though hope were still alive. It could only be that he had told someone about the Gift. Or anyway, about its effects.

The morning after his disclosure, which, he knew, had been prompted by the narcotic, John had regretted his rashness. But he had argued that Jim Braddock was probably trustworthy, for one thing, and for another he hadn't taken the story seriously (on coming later, that afternoon, he had acted as if he hadn't visited in days).

John's sediment regret was over having wept in front of Jim, over having no doubt made the man as uncomfortable as a prince among paupers.

John was sorry about Jim's feelings, but not for his own. Every tear had been as precious as a kind word.

John strolled. He breathed deeply through his nose, taking in aromas. Later he might feel guilty or ashamed for this freedom of spirit, such as it was, poor frail thing. At the moment he would enjoy.

John was glad not only that he had told, but that he had resisted the urge to tone down, sweeten with silence. What he had left out in respect of other effects was of no consequence. That he had nearly been murdered himself by stricken husbands, three times, could, in the telling, only make him seem a romantic figure, falsify. That at least two other husbands had killed themselves was gilding gothic a tale already rich in melodrama.

John came to a stealthy halt, tall-crouch leaning like a fiction burglar. Through the trees he could see a bird. It stood on a rock cleaning and preening, after each fuss with feathers reaching its head high as though to shower in the glory of being handsome.

John smiled broadly. Surprise at this rare act made him gasp. The bird, alerted, flew away.

Feeling an omen of shame, John walked soberly on. He gave stern attention to what he had come out looking for this afternoon, even while his mind was slipping back to outer Boston, the woods on the Carter estate.

He had stolen eggs there, left his seed there, camped and hunted there, failed regularly to lose his virginity there, read Kant there, and decided there to go to Europe. He would become a gentle-eyed, wise philosopher who smoked a pipe on sidewalk cafés while girls gazed upon him and softly touched the back of his hand.

John's parents had not approved. They saw nothing wrong with their hardware business. Nevertheless, hints of being cut off with one red cent proved to be bluster. When his mother retired from living one month after his father's death, John found himself sole heir. Assets sold, the income was enough to live on with care. He could give up his odd-jobbery and go back to Paris from cheaper Spain; stop worrying about money and therefore quit cigarettes (he had never gotten used to a pipe); spend more time on his beloved sidewalk cafés without rousing the waiters' wrath; rent a decent apartment.

At the age of thirty-six John Armitage had felt that he had everything he wanted—except for that one elusive, the gaze of girls. Sex he sometimes had, though never with a woman who stirred him into more than polite arousal. Sex, in any case, was not his drive. His testes were not in charge and never had been. What he desired above all was to be wanted romantically. If it could happen but once he would feel gratified. It didn't have to develop into an affair, one of the body as well as the senses, just so long as he was the object of the lady's profound affections. That once would suffice if not fully satisfy and he could relish the memory forever onwards.

This, it became clear, was not to be.

John went on having the occasional, short affair, plus sturdy friendships with women who wanted nothing more of him than he should listen to how they were suffering in the throes of love.

Unburdening had done them a power of lasting good, John recalled with new understanding as he paused to look down on Shank, a toy village prettily clear in the afternoon light. So would it be a help to confess all the way? Not to a professional, a cleric, there wasn't enough of faith left for that, for any of the rituals, but to your amateur listener, maybe a bartender or an old man on a park bench, someone you would never see again. Someone who would be safe. Safety had to be taken into consideration.

Thinking dully of his crime, and knowing he would

probably never reveal it, John moved on. Absently he had changed his direction from climb to descent, which, presently, he saw. He kept on because underfoot was fresh, untrodden.

Of course, John thought, there was always confession in the form of a confidence, the sharing of a secret. You would do it only with a trusted friend, somebody who had proved such trustworthiness by previous silence. Time would tell.

The trees grew closer together. John swung by the arms from trunk to trunk on the slope. As the downgoing became more of a nuisance he branched to the side. There was an outcropping of rock, house high. Around it John found a room-size patch of land, treeless and level, carpeted with pine needles and cones. There being no evidence of human trespass, the spot had an essence of virginity.

John performed a slow turn centrally, his arms raised at the sides like a prophet on canvas. While telling himself that this would do beautifully, he was acknowledging that although time might pronounce on trustworthiness, it would not necessarily give an insight to response. Whether deserved or not, he wouldn't want to be recoiled from in disgust.

FOUR

As spring fought on, its green forces surrounding and encroaching upon Shank, a fifth column within the settlement appeared to wave a welcome. With their usual contempt of esthetics these weeds grew formless and ugly around cabin, vehicle, and flotsam.

Jim went on seeing Missy secretly in her cabin except for the time when Elsie and five other women did a movie trip to town; he enjoyed having Missy on his own bed. In public he avoided looking at her, which, he felt sure, was beginning to be noticed.

That Jim made no further attempt to tell John about Missy he put down to decency, to his being no kiss-and-teller, not realising that he connected such a telling to the gruesome picture of a grown man crying.

Even though Elsie semi-suspected that the John Brown fatal-attraction story could somehow be part of Jim's possible affair with Rachel, she still turned her head away from the window whenever she heard the motor cycle. Her lack of sex with Jim was of little concern to her at this season, she, along with several others locally, suffering an allergic response to the weeds. That she hardly mentioned her itches and sneezes to Jim gave a consoling satisfaction.

The Milanos' marriage having reached its ultimate falter at the poetry reading, which helped gossip, for interest in John Brown had faded, the wife left triumphantly for

New York in order, she said, to live. The husband, glum, started selling off household goods to raise the cash for his traipse to Mexico. Shank was finished, they both said.

Every other day thereabouts John went up to his place, a three-minute climb from home. Since he daren't sit outdoors by the cabin for fear of being seen by some soft-wandering female, his place formed garden and stoop, yard and patio. He sat, lay, read, dozed. He met wonderful people and had fascinating conversations. In a hidden niche under the huge rock, wrapped in plastic against the damp, he kept a loaded revolver, reading matter, and personal sundries.

Chimneys stopped smoking, peajackets got left off and beards were shortened, women began practicing that chin-drop and indrawn bottom lip prelude to blowing between the breasts. The safety-pin craze died.

Jim never mentioned the fatal-attraction story to its teller, whom he saw often, calling in for a drink or to win a game of Scrabble. That bizarre tale had gone far back in his mind, in fact, sent there not by effort but by the image of John himself: he was so ordinary, unglamorous, and self-effacing, he simply didn't fit with the role he had laid claim to when under the influence of dope.

Missy became convinced that most Shankites now knew of the affair, which made it unimportant when the hints she dropped about Jim failed to get picked up.

The reason Missy didn't outright tell, not even the one who came closest to being her best friend, Rachel, was because that would have been uncool, unShank.

The last of his household goods Jake Milano traded with Store Marsha for ten gallons of wine, with which he intended giving a party to say good-bye to his friends and good riddance to the village, which he blamed for destroying his marriage.

"Slow party," Jim said.

The man addressed, a contender, glanced around with the laziness of an old bitch answering a pup's yelp. Seeing that the speaker wasn't somebody of his own standing or less but one whom he viewed as a major, he sharpened to say gratefully, "It sure is, Jim. By God it is."

"Still, it's early yet."

"There's that, of course. It's pretty damn early."

Like the unemployable threatened with jobs, the twenty-odd people were slouching sourly against the walls of the near-bare room, whose door and windows were open to the soft evening.

Wearing, as was almost every male, plaid shirt and jeans, Jim sipped his wine and gazed about him with a whimsical smile, the man of confidence, stability. It was no act. Jim felt solid and secure, a tree of knowledge in a copse of moron saplings. All in his world was flowing as smoothly as the friendship that can follow passionate love, providing enough time separates the two.

The handful of majors present were grouped by the drinks table.

"Here's Elsie," the contender said, speaking the way a pedant shows off.

Looking around, Jim saw his wife on her way in, walking grandly upright and towing Store Marsha by the hand. They wore what most females in Shank were now wearing, long skirts of jazzy cotton and no bras under plain T-shirts. As though she feared silence, Marsha still bore her collection of jewelry.

Ogling Elsie's breasts, despite having ignored them when they were bare in the bathroom an hour ago, Jim made a decision that pleased him.

Tonight, he would make love to his wife. He would take

her home from here and brush aside those endless complaints about hay fever.

Jim drained his glass as he moved off, heading for the makeshift bar, where his wife and Marsha were getting wine. He stopped as more people came in, one of them being Missy. Between heads he watched her while letting himself be talked at by a nobody.

Missy saw Jim. She returned the usual blind-man glare and from it got the usual pleasure. This made up for her not finding him particularly attractive tonight, just as her continuing frustration over his lovemaking gave her the feeling that she was suffering in her role, secret mistress of a married man.

But in respect of appearance Missy liked reminding herself, as she so often did, that only somebody as truly in as Jim could get away with not having facial hair.

Someone thrust a glass of wine into Missy's hand. She drank with emotional thirst. It had seemed endless, her wait for the evening to come and then for the cabin to get more peopled so she could enter.

Jim, still looking at her, was mouthing words. Concentrating on the repeat, she understood: *We have to be careful*—jerk of the head—*Elsie.*

After nodding that she understood and mouthing back her agreement to be wary, Missy scanned about. No one was watching but she knew how slick people were at quickly looking away.

More guests crowding in behind her, Missy moved on, wafting back merely one of those looks which implied to the newcomers that it was a pity they had missed so much fun.

In the following ten minutes Missy finished her wine and talked to everyone she passed who was of consequence, plus a tourist crasher who gave her a sip from his bottle of rye. He said it fit her mouth nicely. She said, "Now now." There was, she mused happily, a definite salaciousness in the ambience.

Marsha came along with a tray of filled glasses. "Grab one," she said. "If I can drink this rubbish anyone can."

"They say it's a good month," Missy said.

"You're a decorative asset to this village."

"So're you, Marsha, for heaven's sake. You're the sexiest person in Shank."

"I'd drink to that if I didn't have my hands full."

Lifting one of the glasses Missy directed it to Marsha's lips and watched as half the wine got sucked noisily out. They laughed at each other's eyes. Marsha's wet chin Missy dabbed and stroked with a tissue. Her joy was dimmed but slightly when, in glancing sidelong, she saw that the tourist crasher had his back turned.

When Marsha moved on, Missy went the other way, heady and smiling and sure that she looked ravishing. The party was the nicest she could remember.

In the kitchen, where upright orange boxes served as a table, Missy ignored the food's visual aspect and fixed herself a tuna-fish sandwich. She ate with elbows tucked in to avoid being choked by scrimmagers.

Out in the main room, needing to kill the cheap-fish taste, she went to the bar. To the woman beside her she said a cautious "Well, hello."

"Hi," Elsie Braddock said. She filled an extra glass while topping up her own from the jug and slurred faintly that it was unfair to blame Shank for the Milanos breaking up.

"I couldn't agree more."

"I love that skirt."

"Thanks, Elsie. You know, you have terrific posture."

"The broken relationship rate here in Shank is not all

that much higher than the national average, frankly. I worked it out. Thank you."

"To your health."

"And to yours."

They clinked glasses, drank, Missy merely sipping because she no longer had a taste or an emotional need. Humming inside she listened to Elsie's long account of how the Milano marriage had deteriorated.

On seeing beyond Elsie the approach of Jim, Missy stopped telling herself that everybody would be keeping a sly eye on this encounter, wife and girl friend. Suddenly she felt awkward. She seemed to have become ungainly.

After hissing with the rolled eye of panic that she had to take a little pee, meanwhile bobbing with knees and feet together as if about to jump, Missy turned away and slipped off through the crowd.

Elsie smiled affectionately. A nice kid, she thought, if somewhat irrelevant. Why couldn't she be natural? Why couldn't they all be?

Elsie swayed as to her came the urge to tell everyone, one at a time or *en masse,* that they were okay, good, fine and dandy, they could drop their pretences over a cliff, she loved every last one of 'em.

Recalling that she had sometimes had this urge before, but had never obeyed it, Elsie felt both piqued and proud. She giggled and drank.

Jim said, "Hello there, wife."

She turned to him regally in order to demonstrate how sober she was, despite those two gins at the store with Marsha. "Good evening, husband mine."

Between the kisses he pecked on each cheek Jim told her how pretty she looked tonight, which, Elsie thought, he could have told her at home, when she had posed in the doorway before leaving for Marsha's. Did the flattery stem from the gnawings of guilt?

"Rachel's here somewhere, I suppose," Elsie said, surprising herself.

As though puzzled, Jim frowned. "Rachel?" he asked of space. "Rachel?" He stretched up to look over heads. "Rachel?" It was extremely well done.

"Never mind."

"Yes, there she is."

"Naturally."

"She was invited, I guess. Everyone was."

As though she had just declared the garden party open, Elsie glided on with a bountiful smile. Everyone she paused to chat to she told in leaving, "Do enjoy yourself." When at one stage she met Marsha they both burst raucous with laughter, like hometowners who come face to face in Rome. They shrieked, sagged, and crossed their legs.

A while later Elsie saw that she was standing calmly beside Rachel, who had small white feathers sprinkled in her Afro and small black feathers stuck to her T-shirt. She took her wine glass down from her mouth to say, "You're right, sugar. You're the only one with any brains in this upscrewed village of the halt."

At least he chose someone intelligent as well as striking, Elsie mused in defence of all concerned, while knowing beyond question that her husband couldn't possibly be having an affair, he simply wasn't the type. This Elsie found vaguely depressing.

Elsie headed for the kitchen. At the doorway she looked back. Rachel had moved to where Jim leaned on the wall.

"Hello there, Jimsy."

Jim, who disliked variations on his name, said a lifeless "Howdy." He eased himself erect. Elsie having gone out of the room, he was going to move over to have a word with Missy.

Jim turned, went on. He made for Missy, who was offering her glass of wine to Jennifer, who was shaking her head. Jim liked that, the generosity.

"Dance with me, lover."

Jim let the woman edge him in among the half-dozen people oozing on a small patch of floor. His lack of enthusiasm faded as the woman's body wafted before him like part of a copulation rite. On the next dance he forgot that he had planned to make love to his wife tonight and kept manoeuvring so he could see Missy.

Partners came and went in the slow dancing. Jim was starting to tire when he noticed that Rachel had joined the dreamy sarabanders.

"Hi, Rachel," Jim called.

"Hello again, Jimsy."

She came toward him. Over her shoulder he saw Elsie in the kitchen doorway. He smiled on a wink.

Elsie's return smile dropped at blink speed after she had turned away. So they were still together, she thought. That made it half an hour at least. And not only together but dancing, writhing away there as though she didn't know what. Could be he was making a statement: This is my woman.

"Everything okay, Elsie?"

She was back at the table, beside Philip, who had his guitar standing between his legs, safe from the weavers and jostlers. Everything was dandy, she told him.

She went back to sipping wine and talking music, having a quiet fume about Jim and making a sly appraisal of her companion. Presently, her fume faded to its palest.

Nobody Philip was twenty-four, six feet tall, and a classical guitarist with a gift for folk. The girly prettiness of his long fair curly hair was balanced, denied even, by a face of gladiator features.

"Cutest idea I've ever seen," he said, instigated by Elsie touching her ear-ring flowers, again.

"Give you one, if you like."

His touch as light as if over dots on paper, Philip set about releasing one of the flowers. Its stem passed through the lobe hole slowly, making Elsie shiver. She reached up and quickened the job.

"There. Don't thank me."

"You're uneven now," Philip said. "I'll put it back."

"No problem," Elsie said, not liking the way she had reacted to that shiver. Pulling out the other flower she dropped it into Philip's glass. He dropped the first into hers. They laughed and went back to music.

Time passed. How much, Elsie didn't realise until she caught herself in the middle of a vast, jaw-straining yawn. She looked aside, snarled to normal, said, "Time I was in bed."

Philip said, "I'll see you home, Elsie."

"No no, I'm fine. Don't trouble yourself."

He clasped her forearm suggestively. "Believe me, it's no trouble."

Freeing herself with a gentle pull Elsie said she wouldn't dream of it. "Good night. It was fun. Now don't be naughty and follow me."

She went by him, patting his back as she did, skirmished between people, and reached the doorway. On beginning to cross the main room she was aware of Philip close behind her and of a strangely tall Missy sticking up above the crowd.

Her routine of standing on a box to seem way out and as high as a kite was not, Missy acknowledged, working. Nor, now she thought of it, had there been all that many plaudits the last time she had used it.

With her hands on the shoulders of Marsha and Jim, Missy got down. She warned herself against overdoing things in order to look acceptably crazy here. Store Marsha might be drunk, but wasn't so far gone that she couldn't see through a performance. The same with Jim, though he was holding himself together really well.

Picking up the box Missy made a medium production of handing it on high to a nobody and asking that it be put by the wall. She stepped back to re-form a triangle with the garrulous Marsha and chuckling Jim, the while nodding at the undeniable fact that here she was all right, hanging out with two of Shank's firmest majors.

The trio swayed on. Jim stopped chuckling and Marsha said, "If you really know this guy. Listen. If you really know this guy, why don't we go up there and say hello?"

Elsie didn't know precisely how her predicament had come about. At one stage she had been telling Philip in a no-nonsense way that he needn't follow her one more step, she didn't know who the hell he thought he was, and at the next stage here she was in this ridiculous situation.

They were off the hardtop by several yards. The area was illuminated down to dusk from darkness by light from a nearby cabin's thin-draped window. Her bottom against the top of a fence, an ex-chicken run, Elsie stood leaning her trunk back from Philip. He was holding her at the waist and pressing his loins flat to hers—although his were not quite flat, as Elsie was aware, not without interest.

Nevertheless, she thought, no way was this nonsense about to continue. For one thing she was standing here knee-deep in weeds and already could feel a tingle behind her eyes, for a second thing she didn't approve of this type of foolishness, not at her age.

"How old did you say you were?" Elsie asked, whispering on account of the nearby window.

At a similar pitch Philip answered that he was twenty-four. "Come fall. We're about the same age, Elsie."

"Get away with you, you flatterer. I'm older than I look."

"What you look, Elsie, is great."

"I'm twenty-nine," Elsie said, assuring herself that a reduction of four or five years was a woman's right, if not an obligation.

"You're just saying that."

Resisting the pull on her waist that would draw her into an embrace, conscious of the increasing unflatness of Philip's loins, Elsie said she had to be running along now. "If you'll excuse me."

"Let's neck awhile."

"Look. I'm a married woman. Happily married."

"But this is Shank," Philip said. After releasing her waist he took hold of her wrists, which he drew on to bring her forward.

"There's far less fooling around in Shank than you might think," Elsie said. She reflected, felt vaguely a traitor as well as bourgeois, and added, "Until you get to know people."

Philip again drew on her arms, at the same time craning forward kissingly. Elsie shook her head, in part for herself: his breath smelled of tobacco and tuna, kissing a stranger or anyone else for that matter was definitely not on the menu, and in any case she needed to keep her mouth free so she could go on breathing through it, nose closed to the attar of weeds.

With both of them whispering like parents by the cot,

she negatives, he affirmatives, Elsie freed her arms and lifted them out of the way to form a loop above her head. Briefly, her knees dithered in answer to the erotic charge which ran through her at speed.

The same sensation came again as Philip, swift as a nod, using both hands proficiently, shot up the hem of her T-shirt and set it high above her breasts, where it rested snugly, leaving her bare to the waist. Now, not for gold would Elsie have lowered her arms, permitting sag.

Philip slid his hands upward while Elsie, avoiding his eyes, was saying a tight, "You just put that back down at once." He skimmed onto her breasts with hands that were sure and warm. She gasped thoroughly. Sliding clasped hands to the back of her neck she whispered, "You stop that. Someone might see. Stop." She was excited as much by the danger as by the touch.

But her mind was in opposition. Its orders to desist she hissed at Philip. In a gesture of avoidance Elsie leaned farther back. The resulting increase in her feeling of abandonment was so immediate and delicious that she jerked forward again. Philip then tried to kiss her, which she prevented by swinging forward her elbows to frame her face.

Elsie whispered about the danger of being seen. "Even my husband might come along. He'll want an early night, what with going to town tomorrow morning."

"In the morning?" Philip said. "I'll come see you."

Elsie glared at him from between her elbows. "Don't you dare."

"Just a little social call, Elsie."

"Don't you dare come to my house. In any case, at eleven o'clock I might have someone visiting me."

"Me, like," Philip said, laughing.

With one swift, rough lurch she removed herself from

between man and fence and shot down the front of her T-shirt, saying, "Good night."

Philip called out, "I'll see you tomorrow."

In a shouted whisper Elsie threw back, "No you won't." She began to run. She wanted to run, feeling light. As she brisked along the road she was thinking not of Philip, nor of Jim, but of a good hot slippery shower.

Like most man-woman relationships, what had started out so well had become a fatuous nightmare. Jim wished to sweet Jesus he had never opened his big mouth, claiming to know well the man Marsha and Missy had been gossiping about.

In defence, Jim sulked that it really wasn't his fault. Both women were high on wine, which, him being sober, had made him feel out of place, at fault. It was to cancel that, when he joined them, that he had been forced to act a drunken flabbiness and to slur out his claim.

It might not have mattered if, at that moment, Rachel hadn't been passing, and laughed a derisive "Sure you do." That had pressured him into insisting that he knew John Brown as well as he knew anyone in Shank.

If Missy and Marsha hadn't been majors, Jim pursued in the wallow of his sulk, there would have been no need for either act or claim, nor would he have needed to acquiesce when they asked to be taken there, introduced (*if* he really knew the Brown guy, they said). Several times he got them off the subject, but Store Marsha, the drunker of the pair, not only always came back to it but did so with increased scepticism.

It was Missy who had scotched Jim's every timid objection to the venture. Too far?—they would take the footpath short-cut. Too dark?—she had her flashlight. Too late?—the night was a pup on the teat.

"Are we such a coupla dogs, in your opinion," Store Marsha had clinched, "that your antisocial friend's gonna be unhappy?"

Now they were midway up the narrow footpath, a difficult trek even at sober noon. Missy, in the lead, waved her flash while towing Marsha by the hand. Jim came close behind.

Every time Marsha lurched, being in genuine danger of falling, Jim grabbed her, and every time he did she said to quit pushing. On the steps he had to bear her weight, knowing that if he didn't she could slump backwards onto him, as had already happened three times, bringing them both down. Jim had a scraped hand and a sore chin. He was exhausted.

"Forward, men," Marsha panted. "Sorry there."

"That's okay," Missy called behind brightly. "Think nothing of it." True enough, she thought, having her heels trodden on was a small price to pay for being in on this crazy major-type outing. She was so glad she had been able to dispel Jim's doubts about making the trip—it was funny how particular some people could be when they were drunk.

In respect of the outing's aim, Missy had no interest. Present company was all. She would have been quite satisfied, would have marginally preferred in fact, staying at the party and being seen.

They came to another jagged flight of steps. What should have been a minute's climb went on for five. Missy pulled and wobbled. Marsha laughed and lurched and sometimes sat on Jim's head. Jim toyed belligerently with the idea of pretending to twist his ankle, necessitating a return to the village.

At the top of the steps they stood awhile to recover and

listen to Marsha ramble about that time in the old days when she and . . .

Missy gave the kind of chuckles which would make her sound nicely drunk. Jim had no need to act his sag and sway.

"Forward, men," Store Marsha said for the fiftieth time. They went on, still in the same file. For her own homage to repetition, Missy again said she sure hoped the guy wasn't asleep when they got there.

He would not be, as Jim well knew. John was more likely to be eating his lunch, having been out walking or in town or reading most of the previous night. He would be home and stridently awake.

Jim had no qualms about taking two females to see his neighbour. Or rather, the qualms he had initially been visited by had left once he had accepted that the alternative to the venture was a damaging loss of face. John's story about all women falling for him was not, of course, true, Jim knew, and he felt sure that they would all be able to have a good laugh about this escapade. Afterwards.

The trio went on and up. Towing, singing, calling back encouragement, Missy adored herself for being so patient with these two lovely stumbledrunks. She wouldn't forget tonight in a hurry.

"Thank Christ," Jim said to himself in a gasp that was close to a sob when they came at drear length onto level ground. They were behind the Kuzak cabin, which loomed darkly. To the left, a nightlight glow in the bedroom window showed that Elsie was asleep. Lights in the cabin to the right gave notice of John's wakeful presence. Jim experienced the return of a qualm.

Store Marsha pushed on and took Missy's arm, panting, "Forward, men." Missy said, "I sure hope the guy isn't asleep when we get there."

"Sshh," Jim said. "Keep your voices down." That sounded so sober and square that he quickly covered with a laugh. In earnest he began to think of a way out, of not going through with the visit, at the same time feeling safe in knowing that it was too late, but liking himself for the effort.

In the furry silence of heavy breathing they waded through weeds to the lane, there went along right. Jim gave up on outs. Missy, arm in arm with Marsha, found herself growing curious about the person for whom she had previously had not the slightest curiosity.

They came level with the end cabin. Giggling, the women stopped two yards from the door. Jim went by them at a stately pace, like a policeman with dire news. While not happy with what was about to happen, he nevertheless appreciated its inevitability. He halted by the step.

Missy urged Store Marsha forward. As though by arrangement, they separated on reaching Jim, each going to a different side of the door-frame, there to poise like pouncers. Missy put her flashlight off and back in her skirt pocket.

Because the graze on his right hand wouldn't be seen in the gloom, Jim hinted at its existence by knocking with his left. He called out, "John—it's me."

The three people held their breath. From inside came the sound of footsteps, the scrape of a bolt. The door drew in. Looking at Jim, John began a pleasant "Well—"

With a loud return to breathing both women swung around into view. John became as a statue. Jim shook his head. Marsha laughed and Missy laughed. At a snap, John recoiled with wildness growing on his face like a reverse blush. Jim mumbled, "Stop." Marsha began to push inside, laughing, reaching. Missy followed. Jim took a step backwards.

John, still recoiling, raised both hands with an invisible harmonica to his mouth, which was in the shape of dread. The sound he gave was like the whirring of many wings.

Missy and Marsha stopped, in doing so grabbing one another. Missy felt nauseous and in need of support. That the stranger's face had become twisted out of its ordinariness by a weird expression she found disturbing and offensive.

Unawarely Jim took another step backwards. He was hurt by and afraid of the way John looked there in a stiffness with his hands up to his face as though he had a perfect right to be alarming.

When now John flung into action Jim instinctively jerked up protective forearms. But John was only twisting himself around. He went at a semi-run to the bedroom and out of sight. The door slammed home.

Busily, Jim strode forward. "Out," he said in the carrying voice of command. "This is ridiculous." The women turned to him, their faces slipping. He added, as quietly as kindness should be, "Come along, girls, time to go."

After getting them outside and closing the door, he took an arm of each and urged them along the lane. He sighed like a rage of regret. He shook his head in swoops. He tried to think of an explanation.

Although Marsha went on muttering *Jesus* with every other exhale, the name was getting lighter. It rose to a final *Gee* when Missy asked, "What was that all about, Jim?"

Like a girl with a broken heart, Missy was recovering at annoying speed. She would have liked to have extracted more drama from those few awful seconds back there. It was with grateful interest that, following a repeat of her question, she heard from Jim about John Brown's seizures, which came on him without warning every month or so and were the main reason he kept severely to himself.

Cheery and unnauseated again, Missy brought the flashlight from her pocket. "Wow," she said. "Was that wild." She and Marsha hurried into a recap of the entrance scene. Missy hardly noticed when Jim said near his cabin that he would peel off here, he guessed they would be okay with the flash and all.

FIVE

Elsie was less than attentive when, over breakfast, Jim began to talk of last night. Twice she interrupted to say, after a glance at the clock, "Don't forget you're meeting the others at ten."

Only once did she become all-clear, asking whether Rachel had been in on the venture. Jim said, "Rachel? No, just Marsha and that blonde."

Since he not only had an honest look about him, like someone with rotten teeth, but must surely know that the truth would come out through Marsha, Elsie wondered if again she would have to revise her opinion of the affair. She immediately lost interest and looked at the clock.

"So we went up there," Jim said.

Elsie said, "I came straight home from the party." She said it once more before settling to a pretence of involvement with her food and the story of a drunken ramble. She managed disapproval on hearing of the visit to John.

"That was thoughtless of you, hon."

"It was all in the name of fun," Jim said. "But I'll admit he seemed a bit pissed off about it. He stalked into the bedroom. Left us flat."

Elsie tutted and said it was a quarter of ten.

When Jim had gone, Elsie kept her mind busy by singing old songs, the words to which she had to scour about in her mind for, this while washing dishes, tidying around, making the bed, and taking a shower. She dressed in time to a lusty-loud marching song.

Turning in front of the mirror, shoulders relaxed, she heard a knock on the front door. Early yet, the caller could only be a Shankite on the social prowl, some woman who would stay and stay, selling personal problems as avidly as plastic dishes.

Elsie enjoyed tiptoeing across to the door. Hoarsely she said, "I'm sick."

"I don't believe you, Elsie," a male voice answered. It belonged to Philip.

She snatched the door open in offence. "I'm not a liar, dammit. I'm sick. Sort of."

"You don't look it."

"I have a headache."

"You look wonderful."

Head inclined slightly toward raised forefinger, she warned, "I can't let you in."

Philip said, "Don't be like that."

"I'm not being like anything."

"Listen. I was awake for hours last night composing a tune for you."

"How sweet."

Somehow, while Elsie was looking at the way his neck emerged from his collar, Philip came inside. He took her arm like a crony. Elsie found herself being walked in a circle, with Philip humming a version of his composition.

It was a long piece. Making it longer was Philip's insistence on getting every note right, which meant repeats of whole sections. Periodically he said he wished he had thought to bring his guitar.

When Elsie could take no more of circling—her leg on the inner side ached at the hip—she drew Philip to a stop and stood in front of him boldly.

"It needs a lot more work," she said.

"Let me do this last bit."

"No, thank you. I'd much rather hear the whole thing when it's finished and polished."

"You've got something there."

Before she could act in defence, Elsie was in Philip's embrace and being kissed on the lips. She whined an objection. Sliding her hands of protest higher from his chest she felt his shoulder-muscles, which were as thick as she had known they would be. When she took her tongue out of his mouth she said, "No, you mustn't." She squeezed those muscles.

"Let's go in the bedroom," Philip whispered into her cheek.

"It's out of the question."

"Not in the least. No way."

"What makes you think I'll go to bed with you?"

"Your maturity, Elsie," Philip said. "That's what." He separated his words with kisses on her cheek and tightenings of his arms around her waist. "I never met anyone as young as you who was so mature. I guess that's what attracts me to you. As well as you being a beauty."

Elsie was too intelligent to not allow herself to be taken in by what was almost certainly a line. Besides, she knew there was always the chance that Philip spoke in truth, and it would be no strange thing if he did, she being undoubtedly mature and reasonably attractive.

The blame Elsie put on her vanity, however, keeping carnal desire out of it, when she whispered, before kissing him, that bed was out of the question. Her own bed.

During the kiss, with probes being exchanged, Elsie agreeably moved backwards in answer to a gentle urging from Philip, who had picked up the urging from Elsie like a skilled dancing partner.

Shuffling, kissing, they passed through the bedroom doorway and arrived by the foot-rail of the brass bedstead. Philip tried a sideways urge. Elsie shook her head, broke off the kiss long enough to say, "Bed—no."

They began on groping. They kissed, gasped, groped, whispered, conspirators in an act of stealth. From time to time Elsie said, "That's enough." Silent as a breeze she started to urge down towards the thick rug.

It happened swiftly. Philip was strong. Also her body helped, being in the process of bending.

Philip picked her up, stepped around the foot-rail, and dropped her crosswise on the bed.

The air left Elsie's lungs. In defence she was able to do no more than pull at Philip's hair, and that feebly.

By the time Elsie was breathing normally her sensuality had long disappeared, leaving dregs of disgust. She lay with arms down and face turned aside during the attack's remaining seconds.

Through, Philip sagged immobile. He rasped and gulped as he clung to the summit. Elsie thought: We're stuck together. We'll turn back to back. I'll squeal.

Too depressed to be emotional, Elsie said when calm came, in a flat, quiet voice, "Please get up and leave."

Philip mumbled, "What?"

"If you do not leave at once I will tell my husband." To her own ears Elsie sounded strangely formal, as though addressing an inferior. "I mean what I say so you had better go at once."

Philip started to push up. Closing her eyes Elsie felt his removal from her person and the bed, heard his exit from the room and the house. She opened her eyes again. She stared into a corner of the ceiling.

That afternoon, declining sun movement making the peaks seem to be growing taller, John set out on a walk through the trees. He saw little, heard nothing. His body was enjoying the walk.

Following daydreams of sanctuary, the self-made solitudes, John had his mind on the possible charms of prison. He realised that except for accidental criminals—wife murderer, tempted clerk, drunk driver—penitentiary was as much a haven for its inhabitants as were feigned idiocy and military service for those who adopted such a stance or rank. Behind high walls you were fed and clothed, comforted with routine, relieved of all responsibilities, and handed the key to the ultimate in security.

Perhaps then that haven could be used, employed as a massive guard, John thought. Recidivists showed life to be bearable behind the walls, no less than it was for those whose walls were loose smiles or uniforms, and in the right prison for an acceptable, respectable crime, plus the money to pad your way, it could be a life higher than mere bearable.

John asked how you managed to get sent to a penitentiary without being in view. How could you commit a crime, give yourself up or arrange to be caught, spend the jail-time interim, appear in a courtroom, all interspersed with street scenes—and not be seen by women? And if you did win a sentence, how long could you stay free of women visitors?—lawyers, reporters, psychiatrists, a dozen other possibilities.

John shook his head out of exasperation at himself. All this he had been through before, numberless times, the points by now as stale as old air and owning a certain rhythm. After every crisis he went back over the alternatives, from desert island to cave to jungle tent. Nothing within reach of his pocket was feasible, except constant moves.

Unaware of quickening his step, John went on along a level path high above Shank. His features, like a slave wage, were grim but steady. He had come far in spirit from that peculiar minute when the two women had burst in on him, bringing fear and shock. Already he was studying maps, planning a move.

John's disappointment was strong. He had hoped that Shank would be good for many months, maybe even years, since by repute it was the kind of place where an assumed eccentric would be understood, let alone. In the event, the village had lasted some six weeks, two less than the last town, one more than the town before that, three less . . .

Slowing his pace, John sighed. There had been so many changes in the past three years, so much squandering of time. All those intricate arrangements, detailed plannings, bouts of hiding. All those tricks of concealment when travelling or seeing landlords and agents, the crash-helmet, the ski-hood, the bandaged face. All those excuses to new neighbours, by note or telephone or voice over, sounding worse when the neighbour wasn't next door but ten miles away in the nearest shack, for by the mores of country life the greater the separating distance the stronger the need for intimacy, contact.

That John didn't sigh again was because he was sick to death of sighing. He changed direction to get a distracting glimpse of Shank, which soon appeared below as toy roof-tops and trinket cars.

Standing sweaty in the shade of a tree, gazing down with a surprise tinge of fondness, John was undistracted. He reminded himself of the chance that he was still safe, that he had no need to leave this village where his life had been comparatively calm.

First, the two women, obviously drunk, could have been too much so to have seen him efficiently, get him in focus. Next, they could be non-susceptibles. Three, as there had been a hint of carnival in their manner, they could even have been men in female costume—the dark one had certainly had a masculine look while the other had been overly pert and pretty.

Or, John mused wryly, hurt, knowing his hopes to be foolish, maybe both women had since died of the bubonic plague. He laughed with his throat.

In a moment, after going over those hopes again, John set off downward. His place he wouldn't visit today. It could only make him feel worse, him thinking of his plans to spend nights there under the stars this coming summer. Plans now lying in sneery shreds.

With the scratchiness of moral discomfort, John thought about Jim Braddock. Having been the one to call out, Jim would seem to have been part of the ruination scene.

As before, John tried objecting with the facts that there was no ulterior reason for Jim to bring the women, that he had looked sober, had stood back, and had sounded tough in getting the intruders away. The try again failed. Jim Braddock had to be at fault.

However, John couldn't find it in him to think searingly of his neighbour. The blame, he thought, going back to before the visit, was mostly his own. Jim hadn't sold himself as a paragon, as anything, nor had he asked to be allowed to play the part of confidant, to be trusted. Perhaps he even resented being burdened with another man's strange secrets, though it was far more likely that he had dismissed them as the fantasising of a dope smoker.

No, John willingly allowed in order to lose his discomfort, the fault was therefore purely his own. It was due to his conviction, long held, that he was an excellent judge of character, though how he could go on clinging to that straw after it had broken the camel's back he didn't know. Probably it was the comfort in self-delusion, possibly it was the satisfaction in feeling naive, certainly it was the hope that he had been right about Paul Ganieri.

John liked him at once, the first time they met, in the Liberty American Bar on rue Grenoble late one night. Flattery, he told himself without spoiling its effects. We all want to be noticed, remembered, and Paul not only said, "I've seen you before, here and at other places," but backed that by recounting minor incidents—an argument, a spilled coffee. For hours they had talked, deriding a Lord Russell over one drink, lauding a Descartes over another.

Paul, Italian parents, French nationality, German-British education, had spent much of his adult life in India, a student of creeds. He said he was not a mystic, the while smiling as though to encourage disbelief. An observer of the human comedy, is what he claimed to be, though he got no closer to cracker-barrel philosophy than that, and in any case anything trite he might say would have been raised to a level of possible pungency by his appearance.

Over standard slacks and sweater Paul Ganieri wore, orchid in a beer bottle, a kaftan with a hood. The color was grey, the condition scruffy. It went melodramatically with a haggard face of strong features, cheek-bones as thrusting as hunger, eyes darker than the shoulder-length hair, overlong nose curling under at its tip. The beard, greying at one side, was as unnecessary as a feather in a hero's cap, serving only to add more years to the fifty on display. Paul Ganieri had presence, albeit of a decided theatrical nature.

In the early hours he had put a card on the table, saying in his soft, lightly drawled voice, "Where I live. Come at five tomorrow, if you feel like it. I'll introduce you to something a little special."

John came to a snapped halt. Wide eyes as still as his body, he listened to the sounds of passage. They seemed to be coming from somewhere below and to the left, but he knew how these mountain slopes could distort, smother, and magnify noises, or shift them elsewhere like a malicious ventriloquist. The sounds could be from one small bird or several people or a treetop breeze.

What mattered to John most vitally was that they might be from one of those two women; that he was in danger of being seen for the second time.

The sounds were louder.

Obeying his order to move, any direction at all, John went to the right. He darted, crouching. His stomach-muscles were held so hard they ached, as though waiting to be punched. He hoped he wouldn't panic.

Because of the noise he was making himself, despite trying to go with care, John could no longer hear the other sounds. He swung his head like a gate in a gale in order to see every way almost at once. That he saw no one increased his worry.

On a steep patch he gave up on the care, sat, and let himself slither downward. Upright again, moving, he started taking off his windcheater so as to use it over his head.

A voice in front called, "That you, John?"

They walked down one behind the other on a path through the trees, which suited Jim, for, being in front, John had his face out of sight. It hadn't mattered before, a minute ago, during his explanation to John of having come to see him at the first opportunity and, finding him out, having looked for him up here, since that was the truth.

"See, I wanted to tell you about last night," Jim said. "To set you straight."

"I see."

"I wouldn't blame you for thinking badly of me. It must've looked real funny."

"It did, yes."

"Anyway, what happened was, I was at a party. Those two women were there as well."

Sharply, John asked, "How drunk were they?"

"Very," Jim said. "Really wiped. And that was the problem." He told himself everything was all right, he had it made. "See, when I left they got the idea I was going to another party. So they followed me."

"You were coming to my place?"

"I knew you'd be awake, even though it was late."

"Of course," John said in a neutral tone.

"That was the situation, John."

"You must've heard them behind you."

"Sure. But I thought they'd give up. But they didn't. They came right onto your house, though I'd been telling them there was no party, to give up and go away."

"They were there when you knocked."

"I thought I'd finally convinced them," Jim said, offering a hand at each side, which, he expected, would look effective from behind.

"You got the wrong impression."

"They seemed to straighten out. In fact, they were moving off when I knocked and shouted. They would've been gone if you hadn't opened the door so quickly. Too bad you did that. Even so, I'm sorry. No kidding."

"Can't be helped, Jim. It's all right. I don't think badly of you."

"I'm glad you let me explain about this, John. I mean, how stupid if our friendship should be broken by a couple of dumb tourists."

"Oh yes?" John said, to play the words his voice taking on a different timbre. "Tourists?"

"Pure rubes," Jim said. "They'd crashed the other bash. In fact, I'd been asked to get rid of 'em, so I didn't mind at first when they followed me a ways."

"I understand."

Past the last tree Jim stepped down onto the lane. Turning as John joined him he said, pursuing unnecessary defence, "It really wasn't my fault."

"No no, forget the whole thing."

"And let's face it, I didn't believe that story you told me."

"It's bizarre, I admit."

Like a middleman determined to keep his position, Jim inclined the other way with, "But as Elsie says, the fact that you told something so outlandish showed how serious you were about wanting to be let alone."

"Tourists," John said, tapping five fingertips on his chest. "They were tourists."

"Pittsburgh, I think they said. You'll never see 'em again, very likely."

"Thank you."

Feeling once more that he had put himself down too much, Jim said, "Not, of course, that it honestly matters. I mean, does it? Honestly?"

"You're talking about the story?"

"Right."

After John had brought Jim to a stop by touching his arm he settled himself to a spread-leg stance with nods, on some of which he closed his eyes like a mother showing patience.

"That story," he said, "is true. As true as these mountains. I'll have to make it absolutely clear to you, Jim, impress the truth of it on you, so you won't, accidentally, allow a repeat of what happened last night."

Looking away from the continual on-off contact of eyes with its suggestion of intimacy, Jim laughed his awkwardness. "Well, I don't know what to say to that."

"You don't have to say anything."

"I mean, let's face it, I'd hate to think you were some kind of nut."

John said, "It is possible, yes, that I'm out of my mind. That the whole thing was created by my sick imagination. Wouldn't that be wonderful?"

"I guess," Jim said, moving on. "The sun's gone." He felt chilled as well as awkward.

John walked at his side. In a moment he said, "Clearly you don't believe in things of an occult nature."

"Can't say I do. You do, though."

"I don't know if that's right, as a matter of fact," John said. "You know, there might be another explanation altogether for the Gift."

"That's what you call this deal of yours? Doesn't sound like much of a gift to me."

"Completely the reverse. Gift's just a name. Curse would suit better."

The quietly dull way John spoke made Jim ruffle himself to brightness like a waking jester. He asked, "And it just grew on you?"

"Let's say I acquired it."

"Too bad you can't unacquire it."

"I have an idea there is a way to pass it on," John said.

"But even if I knew what it was, would I be able to bring myself to do it? I don't know."

"Don't you have an enemy?"

"I'm not sure I have a friend. Except you."

Pleased, Jim sympathised, "Your lousy Gift hasn't done you one bit of good, has it?"

John flapped an arm against his side. "It's taught me compassion." Another flap. "It changed me from a cool son of a bitch to someone who cares. You have to suffer for that." Another flap. "Compassion without having suffered is an act."

"You're okay, John. You're a nice guy."

As though he hadn't heard, John said, "That change is what's kept me going. Supported me. Especially in those terrible, terrible times. Tragic times. I've been searching for a way to use the Gift to positive ends. To help people. I've spent thousands of hours on the subject. I never got anywhere. There is no way. I think I've accepted that now. I think I've given up. I'll probably stick to my resolution to end it all, one of these days. There's no reprieve in view as far as I can see into the distance. I would have before, ended it, except for that search, as well as lingerings of religion. But one of these days, yes. Fortunately I don't fear death."

As well as chilled, Jim was beginning to get bored. Also he had the recognised fear that he might be in for another assault of tears.

After telling John not to worry, things always worked out in the end, he said, "Come on, let's step on it. I'll give you a game of Scrabble."

For a week after the short, strange call on John Brown, Missy enjoyed telling people about it, or anyway, telling about being in the company of Jim Braddock and Store

Marsha. If she happened to be in the bar at the same time as Jim, she referred to their outing loudly, once with a hand to her brow to express the awesome. She did similarly on each of her near-daily stops in the store, if customers were present; if not, she talked of other matters, having realised that Marsha found John Brown uninteresting and the drunken event an embarrassment.

Jim too appeared unwilling to talk of Brown or the visit, even when Missy had him in a pre-coital embrace, which was the nicest part of their sex, wherein she could float on the tang of anticipation.

Other majors seemed to have just as feeble an interest in the hidden newcomer, save for morbid curiosity about his seizures, and there was no value for Missy in talking about him to other locals. Feeling that she had made her social point, she dropped the topic.

Her silence, however, gave John Brown more prominence in her mind, as if due to him no longer being able to get out through her mouth. Often she relived those confused seconds on his threshold. The reaction he had produced was one of the weirdest she had ever seen outside of a movie. The kind of behaviour you didn't expect from real, everyday people. It was that, the reaction, which brought Missy, finally, to the conclusion that John Brown could be somebody famous.

Seizures had probably not had anything to do with it, she thought. That was just a cover. The man had acted that way out of fury at being discovered, at having his precious anonymity spoiled.

Missy's trouble was, she hadn't recognised Brown. Nor did it help when she tried remembering what he looked like, for she could only conjure up non-descript features under their writhing.

But had it been different with Marsha?—she wondered.

Had she, belonging to an older generation, recognised the newcomer at once? Marsha, on afterthought, had acted oddly, as had Jim, who, of course, would have known all along his close neighbour's true identity. So was that why he and Marsha were reticent on the subject—being protective of a respected celebrity?

Missy was stimulated, unaware that she considered it better to be so than to feel slighted, left out, uninformed by those in the know; feel she wasn't yet quite the major she thought she nearly was.

Her stimulation was only partly feigned, however, since she, like many people, equated fame with godliness. Missy worshipped household names as faithfully and as purely as the savage gave his adoration to a tree. Without difficulty she was able to understand why some individuals were impelled to attempt the impossible or assassinate a world figure.

Missy decided she would have to have another look, good and close, at this John Brown in heavy quotes to see if she could recognise the face. The task might be easy without the mask of fury. How she would do it was, she would go and apologise for that silliness the other night, when she had been forced to accompany her drunken friends.

Or, Missy reasoned, as it wasn't likely he would open the door, and as Jim had mentioned that John Brown took a daily walk, late afternoons, she would go up beyond his cabin and wait in the woods. She would create a nice accidental meeting. She would do it at once.

Somebody groaned and another voice said, "We got ten minutes left, if it's all the same to you."

"Cramp," Missy lied on coming back to now, seeing the uniformed Shankites sitting around her with their sketchpads and drawing-boards.

"You want to take five? You can add it on later."

Wearing the martyr's selfish smile Missy said she would continue. "The pain soon goes." After standing briefly she resettled in her pose on the tall stool.

Missy began to play with possibilities in respect of John Brown. For the rest of the sitting he was a violinist of international renown. She accompanied him on a tour of the Orient while dressing, while collecting five dollars from each artist, on leaving, and while making her way up the short-cut.

Before climbing the final flight of steps, which would have brought her in view of the three cabins, Missy turned right and took an obliquely upward trudge. She wore that smile again. She was well away from the last cabin when it did come into sight, far enough to be safe if she sat down. She sat.

Fifteen minutes later, with John Brown a famous stamp collector who never travelled, Missy decided because she was tired of waiting that he wasn't going to take his walk today. Her second decision was that it would be simpler to step out from behind her pride and ask Marsha.

When Missy walked into the store the first person she saw was Jim's wife, who, she realised, would be an even better prospect than either of the other two, pridewise. She would be sure to know the score regarding her neighbour.

Elsie looked less her cheery self, it seemed to Missy, as though she saw not the goods but the approach of middle age.

"Hello, Elsie."

"Hi," Elsie said. "How's everyone down your way? Rachel and everybody."

"Fine, I guess," Missy said uncertainly, but next saw the free cue. "How's everyone up in your neck of the woods?"

"We're just dandy."

"I guess you heard about our call on John Brown, right? Me and Jim and Marsha."

Elsie nodded. "Someone did say that you'd mentioned it around a couple of times. I hope it doesn't happen again, the visit. The poor man wants to be left alone, seems to me."

"Sure, I understand that. Famous people get bothered all the time, I know."

Elsie asked who was famous and Missy said, using the name because it had just come up, "Rachel, I think it was, told me your John Brown's a celebrity. She didn't say what at."

Elsie nodded as slowly as if she were digesting news, one item after another, all drab. With the last nod gone she said, "Don't let this go a step further, but there's a rumour that old JB is a top Ku Klux Klanner." With the raised finger of caution, she turned away.

Missy didn't know whether or not to take Elsie seriously. Either she would ask Jim straight out, she thought, or she would go up to try to meet John Brown again tomorrow.

Like its neighbours on that hushed, decrepit street, the house had an air of disdain, as though to ward off pity for the unhidable fact that its spirit had long ago been broken. This continued inside, where only the high ceilings' sculpted plaster retained its immaculate form, a careful duchess aloof to the rabble below.

Long, narrow, tall, the main salon had six worn couches from differing style reigns, a floor of tiles beautiful despite their cracks, and tapestries which John suspected of hiding damp or decay. Closed shutters backed the French windows, making for dimness.

Potentately, Paul Ganieri and John had a couch each. Between them stood a small round table whose cloth's tassels touched the floor. Central was a saucer of liquid, into which the host eased a handful of crystals. Up rose a vapor, gentle as swamp mist.

"Inhale at will," Paul Ganieri said after leaning back from a savour. "It will do you no harm."

The narcotic was sensuously mild, John found. It gave him none of those moments of apprehension, even anxiety, which came at times in cannabis-induced states. He enjoyed the casual ambience, he saw less pretension in his host, he appreciated the conversation as it went languidly from politics to tapestries, from good cheap restaurants to love.

John said, "More has been written on love than on any other theme. Almost. In the index in books of quotations you'll find it equals death in section length."

"Aptly, I should think."

"Why is that?"

Ganieri said, "Falling in love is a kind of death. You have to come back from that to own yourself again."

John was impressed with his new acquaintance.

He became more so on his next visit, two days later. Paul Ganieri, suggesting coffee, tapped a spoon against the steaming saucer to send through the house a sharp, clear cry.

"To finish," he said, going back to his anecdote about Sartre, whom he had prefacely said he had met often—"Though we were not friends, by any means. I was simply another of those who hovered, moths at the flame."

John was liking again the honesty of that while smiling at the anecdote's curtain when he heard sounds of approach. He looked around.

Possibly it was envy, John reasoned afterwards, that

held him back from granting Marie the title of beauty, unconditionally, or it was only her youth that brought the title to mind. He did know she would be a breathtaker in garb more glamorous than her shirt and jeans, did find gratifying her natural grace and smiling shyness, did feel rewarded in looking on her dark waist-brushing hair and the dark deer eyes.

Marie's every move and glance seemed to state that she was in love with, or had a youngster's fierce crush on, the man who sat there in so lordly a fashion, treating her if not with indifference then as though she were a sister.

Girl gone after fetching coffee, John asked, "Is Marie an actress?"

"No. She has no job."

"Actually, Paul, what I meant was, did you hire her to put on that performance?" His suspicion, he saw at once, was probably unfounded, unless the host was himself an actor of high skill. Paul Ganieri looked bewildered.

John said, "Pardon my cynicism, but her love for you is so up front I thought it might be an act."

"But why should it be?"

"I thought it might be a routine of yours to impress visitors."

Ganieri said a cool "Oh, I see."

To cover an awkward silence John hurried into the telling of Dali's reputed habit of unburdening himself of props when callers had gone.

The host said, "Marie is the daughter of a cleaning woman. She lives here. As a matter of fact she could be acting when she claims to love me. She gets free lodgings, after all."

"But you don't believe it's an act."

"I know it isn't."

"You're a very lucky man, Paul. She's stunning."

Ganieri said, "A beautiful child, a willing handmaiden, a fervent mistress."

Accusingly John said, "You're not in love with her."

"I have more sense."

"Don't tell me you can control your emotions."

"They can be influenced, if not controlled. That's enough."

"So what about the future? You and Marie?"

"She will not, of course, love me forever. She'll be spared in time."

"You can't know that."

Paul Ganieri nodded. He said, "In ninety-nine cases out of a hundred romantic, passionate love dies young. It is a child. It has a child's innocence. And, as a child begins to lose that at the age of perhaps two, develop cunning, so does love after two years begin to lose its innocence, blindness."

"This is an old topic with you, isn't it?"

"It is. I mean no boast when I tell you that many women have been in love with me."

John smiled. "And for my part, I mean no complaint when I admit that not one woman has ever given me her love. I mean a heartfelt lament."

"You're young yet," Paul Ganieri said. "Now let's get to a new topic from the old."

On John's subsequent visits to the invalid house Marie always put in an appearance. Once she spent an hour sitting with the men, adding an occasional word, rarely taking her eyes off her lover. She never inhaled the narcotic. Nor, during two visits, did John. Lack made scant difference. He was still impressed, fascinated, and envious. The last had most strength. Sometimes his chest ached in response to the way Marie looked at Ganieri. It wasn't the girl herself who hurt, John easily staying romantically aloof, it was the luster of a devotion which reached noonday force in its intensity.

One night, coming across Paul Ganieri in the upstairs bar at the Liberty, John, woozy with drink, was tempted to challenge him to prove Marie's love, to say, "Order her to sleep with me." Instead, finding that he accepted the love as true, he confessed the fume of his envy.

He ended, "This isn't the first one for you, either, dammit. There've been others. All your life."

"No," Ganieri said. "Only since I've had the Gift."

"Gift? What's that?"

"Nothing nothing. Coming tomorrow?"

When Elsie first saw the lower Appalachians she felt safe. They were so like the peaks in her sole recurring dream, which she had been having since puberty and which, she came to recognise, only played itself for her in times of stress. In it she was sitting by a mountain lake. Nothing ever happened. She simply sat contented in a peace that had the essence of eternity.

By studying maps and taking hiking trips Elsie tried to find her secret body of water. She failed. She had no disappointment, her love of the Appalachians wasn't spoiled, and her search she gave up happily on learning that it was pointless. In the dream that came after she discovered she was not going to have children, a voice from somewhere behind her whispered that she was sitting by the Lake of Wasted Tears.

"I was thinking of taking a siesta, Els."

"Go right ahead."

"Why don't you join me?"

"I'm not tired, hon."

"Well, sleep isn't exactly what I had in mind."

"Oh."

They were doing the dishes from Sunday lunch, Elsie drying. Passing her another plate Jim said, "Must be weeks."

"Really? That long?"

"So how about it, Els?"

Elsie found the proposition vaguely disreputable. This she saw as related to cheating, for ever since her own adventure she had believed consummately in the truth of Jim's affair with Rachel. She avoided thinking that her present response could be due to a feeling of being polluted, that her soiling by Philip should not be passed on.

"I'm going to set up shop down below."

"Isn't it a bit early for that?"

"Summer's almost here. You coming?"

"Not in the mood," Jim said in the grating tone he used when he was entering a sulk.

"Fine," Elsie said. "This one's on me." Racking the plate she strode out of the kitchen before Jim could persist, perhaps trap her with sentiment, or before she could trap herself with knowing how nice it was with Jim so long as she played disinterest for most of the way. She started to gather pictures, materials, campstool.

Within thirty minutes Elsie had laid out the show, pitch of a pavement artist gone West. Twenty crayon drawings were posed roadside against flora, enabling Elsie to sketch from reality as she sat in attendance.

With one reservation, she was pleased with her gambit: Philip might show up. Although it was ten yards to the first cabin, with the village core beyond that around a bend, out of sight, someone could mention in Philip's hearing that Elsie was showing this afternoon. He would be sure to come along.

Elsie hadn't talked to Philip since his assault, eleven days and some hours ago. She had kept out of his way.

When once he came to the house, Jim down at the bar, she had pretended to be out, peering at him from behind the drapes and thinking she must have been out of her mind, he was so unspecial.

Philip's possible telling about the coupling to somebody was for Elsie a minor worry. It would not be spread as an item, to get to Jim, as no one would believe it of her, even in Shank, where bad news was preferable to the good—not because locals were themselves corrupt but because the bad made for more conversation, as well as supplying a reason for letting the poison of insularity run out.

What did worry Elsie was that when she finally met up with him Philip would make a scene and during it fritter away what had happened. Hereabouts there were few scenes that failed to get saturation peddling.

An hour passed. Locals strolled out to visit, tourists drove by as sparsely as slow swallows. Elsie sketched and joined the chat. By asking adroit questions she learned that Philip was in the bar.

Another hour passed. A couple on pedal bicycles bought one of Jim's drawings. Elsie grew nervous, sketched badly, began to scratch herself.

Visitors turned their talk on newcomers, idly. One woman said, "You heard what they say about that John Brown? They say he's Ku Klux Klan."

Elsie looked up from her sketch-pad to stare into space. She mused that if people here were so hungry for news they would believe a joke, they would believe anything. It was time for action.

The woman whom Elsie chose to ask to mind the pitch came weekends from her town penthouse to wear old clothes and straggle her hair. She agreed at a snap. Elsie left. When she looked back at the bend, the woman was sitting with the sketch-pad tenderly upright against her breasts like a layette.

Inside Gustav's, a dozen Shankites took up space at the bar while another group, tabled in a corner, cackled the end of an elsewhere lunch. No meal in Shank was judged a hit unless the hosts could say, "We finished up in the bar."

Elsie put her shoulders back to move into a place at the bar next to Philip, whose eyes she ignored, saying, "Glass of water, please." During the serving she was aware of having a conversation with Florence about the pitch. She was annoyed to hear herself say she had sold three drawings. She was against that kind of thing. Normally she would have said two.

Florence gone, Elsie said aside in a light tone, "Now listen, Philip. I'm glad I caught up with you finally. You're a hard man to corner. I wanted to explain about last week."

Because they were strictly faithful to their marriage vows, Elsie said, she and Jim had this agreement. Once a year they could do exactly what they wanted for twenty-four hours. "I wanted you." It had worked out beautifully. "And it was great that you understood my particular need—playing the semi-victim." She had known when she first saw him that he was a man of experience. "I'm sorry I won't be able to make love with you again."

The rest of it consisted of not listening to Philip's comments, given with the anxious face people wear to discuss literature, while talking over them about her pitch. She slapped his back heartily in farewell.

Feeling regret, and wondering if she should nag Jim to take up bodybuilding, feeling proud, and asking herself how come she was so courageous and smart, Elsie left Gustav's with an erect stride.

Once along the road she indulged in a series of skips.

She was eight years old and music class had let out. Why she stopped skipping was due to a niggle: Yes, but having broken the ice, committed her first act of adultery and had it work out smoothly, would there be other men in her future? Elsie imagined it would be exciting. She was convinced it would be sad.

At Paul Ganieri's house, declining to lean over the saucer, John cut to the point he had been honing since last night in the Liberty: possession of a knack, skill, force. As possibilities he had shifted from drugs to hypnosis to blackmail, with a strong preference for the first.

"What did you mean by the Gift?"

Ganieri said, "I must have been drunker than I realised if I mentioned it."

"I was drunk myself. But please tell me what you meant."

The answer didn't come straight, clean. It was wrapped in the ramblings and convolutions which the narcotic created and which John noticed only when he himself hadn't inhaled the fumes. But eventually there was a statement.

Paul Ganieri had the power to make a woman fall in love with him. That was the Gift. It was a mental factor, involving no external influences or aids. He had been in possession of it for seven years.

After a pause, during which he clenched his fists under the table, John said a terse, "I don't believe you."

"That's quite all right by me."

John relaxed. "Sorry. I take that back."

Paul Ganieri said, "It was expected."

"What I ought to have said was I find it impossible to believe. Incredible."

"Do you believe the Indian rope-trick?"

"No, though I've never completely *dis*believed."

"A standard attitude," Ganieri said.

"But where does the boy go when he disappears up the rope?"

"That, my friend, is what Eastern philosophical mysticism is all about."

John performed the expected, a poignant smile. "When can I start learning?"

"It would take you more years than seven," Ganieri said. "Forget it. Stay on your own course." He lifted the spoon. "Now it's time for coffee."

At home, alone, he was nearly always alone, John found that he was willing to consider the absurd. *There are more things in Heaven and Earth,* he quoted to himself time after time, until it became so trite he believed it. But that, he argued, was for the supernatural, not the ability to turn on at will an irresistible power of attraction. Reason won.

John nevertheless gave ear to the goblins of his mind over the following days, the while fighting an urge to see Ganieri again. He talked to mutual acquaintances. They failed to respond to his hints about a Gift, they could only say with certainty of the shadowy Paul Ganieri, after giving him a good character, that he had been seen with some sensational women.

John clung to his fading scoff. Logic, he knew, admitted, pointed out repeatedly, was being undermined by his emotional need and romantic hedonism. He shook his head at the insanity of Ganieri's story and nodded that so many eminent Westerners believed in an unsupported rope and a disappearing boy.

What did most to take John to acceptance of the Gift as at least a possibility was his realisation, with a curiously strong lunge of disappointment, that, yea or nay, he would not at his age be prepared to go through a decade of study. Fruition thus abnegated, the Gift became less of a threat.

He went back to see Paul Ganieri. Getting no answer, he left in a rage that seemed divided between a thirty-minute journey for nothing and Ganieri's pretentiousness in refusing to have a telephone: he had said they were the wedge-end of civilization at its most mundane. John slept badly.

The following day Ganieri was home. "You've been ill, I imagine," he said as they sat on couches at the round table. "You look worn."

John said he was fine. "I've been thinking about your Gift. I'd like you to tell me more. I'm intrigued."

"Are you saying you believe me?"

"I wouldn't go as far as that. But then, I'm a cynic of almost professional standing."

Paul Ganieri indicated the saucer. "Shall we?"

"Not for me, thank you," John said. "I'd like to hear about your power."

Leaving the saucer alone Paul leaned back with his hands raised as a shrug. "What's to tell? It's there. I've used it. But I don't think I've used women. I'm not the type."

"Has the power ever failed?"

"Never. It can't fail."

John said, "It must've affected your life a great deal these past seven years."

Paul Ganieri said he didn't know about that. "Perhaps my life would have been fairly similar without it."

"Surely not."

"I have, I admit, obtained money with the Gift. However, it was only enough for my wants and comforts. I am not financially ambitious."

"And if a person studied for say ten years he could learn or acquire this power?"

"That's not certain. He might, he might not. Possibly if he studied with only that goal in mind, it would elude him."

John said a flat "I see."

"I wish I hadn't told you about the Gift."

"Yes, it bothers me, that's true. I've always been drawn to the concept of perfection."

Paul Ganieri said, "Perfection doesn't really exist, you know. It's merely a label."

Not wanting to get sidetracked John asked, "Are you the only man in the world with this power?"

"I doubt it. But I don't know."

"And any others, would they all be post-graduates in Eastern thought?"

"Well, I suppose some would have taken the short-cut."

Slowly, the returned wanderer who wonders why everything has shrunk, John looked around the room. He nodded at Paul's offer of coffee and gave a smile of recognition to the chime of spoon on saucer and, when she entered, rose a token space from the couch for Marie, as he always did out of respect for her potent devotion; these while excitedly savouring the host's words.

It seemed an hour until they were alone again, until John could lean forward over his cup and say, "All right, Paul. Tell me about the short-cut."

"You wouldn't be interested," Ganieri said. "Not one man in a million would be."

"Tell me. Please."

Ganieri spoke, John listened. When it became clear that the short-cut toll was the taking of a human life he began to lean sideways in agreement that yes, he would not be interested.

SIX

Afterwards, Jim would tell people, "I was sketching, waiting for Elsie to get lunch, when I saw this shadow cross the light from the window. I looked out and saw the woman going by. Wish I'd gone outside. I might've been able to change things."

The moment he saw her Jim knew the woman was not acting in a normal manner, unless normally she had the tension of an athlete about to fling herself at the high-jump. Her walk said so, the set of her head said so, and her face said so even in profile. Then she was past.

Jim put down his blank sketch-pad, went to the window. Carrying a purse to match her outfit in grey suede, poignantly creased silver at the back, the woman could have been a doctor or grocer's wife or waitress.

She could even, Jim told himself with a nervousness he didn't understand, be an old Shankite come back to see where she had played in pre-straight days.

Jim knew he was wrong there. Visiting ex-Shankites always either bore shyness like a placard or had the jocularity of an actor when he tells why he had accepted that awful part, long ago, when he was so inexperienced.

The woman passed the Kuzak place. She could only be going to John Brown's, Jim reasoned, since it seemed unlikely she would want to see the quarry or simply be taking a walk.

About to call Elsie from the kitchen, Jim went against it

because there was nothing out of the ordinary to show her, just the back of a woman. He sidled to the door, which he opened with his mouth wide to encourage quietness, stepped outside with delicate caution, and moved toward the cabin corner.

Slanting off the lane at a slower pace, the woman went to the far cabin's window. Her try at seeing in was brief. She moved on to the door.

Now, as though a victory were in sight, Jim felt more excited than nervous. After seeing the woman knock, hearing the sound faintly, he sank down behind a clump of weeds. They were turning brown in death.

The woman listened bird-like. She knocked again. She waited. As if in response to an answer, she grew taller and leaned a hand on the door. She talked, her voice floating back as a murmur.

Jim stayed on in his squat. Deciding on not making a dash for the Kuzak place, to be nearer, to hear, he made do with easing forward with his head half turned. The woman's words were still unclear, but the timbre had meaning. It seemed to be one of supplication.

Over the following minutes, while Jim gradually became jaded, making several false starts to get up, leave, the woman knocked and spoke. Her tone changed to threatening, returned to the lilt of wheedle.

With a gasp, Jim twitched back when the woman took a gun out of her purse. He landed in a sit. Scramblingly he got forward again onto his knees. The woman had the nose of her gun touching the door. She was talking urgently.

Jim had no awareness of nodding, of needing to convince himself that here he was, witness to a bizarre and dangerous happening, a part of it.

It was with almost a pang that he saw the woman withdraw her gun from the door and put it inside her jacket. Next he cried out in shock as, at the same time, he heard the shot and saw the woman jerk backwards.

Her arms lifted, gun and purse came free, she fell over onto her back in the dust. She settled, lay still. Jim knew she was dead.

He got up like an old man. His eyes flicked everywhere except at the woman and when he was fully erect he kept his head lowered, as though to reduce the chance of being seen. He turned, walked neatly back and inside the cabin, slammed the door, and went to his chair at the table. He sat.

Elsie looked in. "Oh, it's you."

"Yes."

"Did I hear a shot a minute ago?"

"Yes."

"They get closer all the time."

"Yes, it was a shot."

Elsie came out of the kitchen quickly. "What's wrong? You look terrible. You look white."

Head still lowered slightly, Jim peered up at her with, "I just saw a woman kill herself."

Elsie gave the ghastly smile of incomprehension. It began to fade when Jim had said for the fourth time that he had just seen a woman kill herself.

"Who was she?"

"A stranger."

"Where?"

"Outside John's. She had a gun."

Elsie pointed at him. "I heard the shot." She came to stand behind him and put her hands on his shoulders. "You all right?"

"It was kind of a shock."

"Of course, darling. What did you do?"

"Nothing."

"We'd better go see. If you feel all right."

"I'm okay. It was kind of a shock."

Elsie left, went out. Jim got up and followed. He felt dull, unsurprised. This didn't change when he came up beside Elsie outside and she said, nodding along the lane, "I thought you said she did it outside John Brown's."

Looking at the woman, now lying opposite the Kuzak place, but in the same position as before, purse and gun nearby, Jim said, "She did. He must've moved her."

"Who?"

"John."

"That's insane."

Jim said, "She's been moved."

"All right."

"I mean it, Els."

"Did you examine her?"

"No. I told you that."

"Come on," Elsie said. At a female run, awkward, she went to the woman and there knelt at her side. Jim followed slowly, stopped nearby, stood with his face semi-averted.

Elsie rose with, "Yes, she's dead. Poor soul. She can't be more than thirty."

"It's a shame."

"And what now, Jim?"

"I don't know."

"First," Elsie said, "we'd better get this straightened out with John Brown." She made to move in that direction.

"No!" Jim snapped, on the instant becoming animated.

"What?"

"Don't look at him, Els. You mustn't."

They stared at each other as though at pause in an

argument. Jim shook his head. Elsie said, "Well, I don't know."

"I mean it."

"All right, hon."

With both hands Jim rubbed his face, stroked back his hair, and briefly held his neck. Although he still felt mostly dull, his surprise had gone. He went closer to Elsie but avoided seeing the woman's upturned face.

He asked, "What'll we do?"

"We have to report this. Call to town from the store."

With his head lowered again Jim said softly, "We could move her as well."

"What did you say?"

"We could move her someplace else."

Also speaking quietly Elsie said, "But why?"

"To let someone else find her."

"Yes, but why?"

"Well, to keep us out of it," Jim said. "It's none of our business. Why should we get involved?"

"No one's getting involved. We're just making a call."

"John moved her. If it's good enough for him it's good enough for me. That's what I say."

Elsie took his arm and gave it a pat. "Are you sure it happened at his place?"

Feeling guilty, Jim put on a blank expression. "Why would I lie about it?"

"I have no idea. I'm not thinking straight."

"Look, Els. John moved her and he knows what he's doing. He's been through this before."

Again they stared at one another, drawing back slightly from proximity. This time Jim nodded. He said, "Yes, I guess I believe it."

"His story?"

"Yes. I have to."

"Women in love with him? Suicides and murders?"

"Yes, dear. Yes."

"I'll think about that when the time comes," Elsie said. She looked down. "But this is terrible. My God. This is awful. A woman just *killed* herself."

"I know," Jim said. "It's a shame."

Elsie forced down her rising emotion. This, she glared at herself, was no time for pity. She had to be strong. Someone had to be strong around here.

Jim said, "I need a drink."

"So do I."

"First, though, we have to settle about moving her."

In defence of her husband Elsie mused that he was only copying someone else and that he was, after all, in a state of shock, probably. She said:

"No, Jim. As it is now, it's nothing to do with us. We'd really be involved if we started interfering."

"We're already involved."

"We might leave clues. We might be seen. We could even get accused of murder."

Jim said he needed that drink. Elsie asked, "How about if you went by yourself to talk to John Brown?"

"Not right now."

"I don't see why not."

"Be no point. He'd only deny knowing anything about it. He might not even be in, or have been in before."

"So who moved the body?"

"John, I guess," Jim said with the satisfaction of a moron. He moved away homeward.

Fanning her mouth with relief at having won in the question of moving the woman, Elsie followed. She caught up in order to pat Jim's arm again. That she had a priority for her concern was a blessing.

Inside, while Jim walked around the table, Elsie got out rye and poured two shots. She had a moment of astonishment—a woman was lying out there dead—before bringing Jim to a halt. She gave him a glass. They sipped politely, like strangers at the home of a new friend.

Jim said, "Listen, Els. About this call."

"Yes, hon?"

"When you go to the store to make it, be careful what you say. You know?"

"When I go to the store, be careful. I see."

"What you say to the cops on the phone, I mean."

"You'll stay here and guard the body?"

"The thing is, Els, I'm not going to say I saw the actual shooting. There's no need."

With a hint of the plaintive, Elsie said, "Jim, you're a witness. That's important."

"It makes no difference to that woman out there. For me, I'd be into it ass-deep. Statements, the inquest, pushed around by cops, back and forth to town. No, thanks."

Elsie poured the rest of her drink into Jim's glass. She would have wiped his nose if she could. "What'll you say then?"

"Nothing," Jim said. "When you call, just tell them we heard a shot, went outside, and saw this body. A stranger. We didn't touch a thing. We know nothing about it."

"Why not simply tell the truth?"

"Because it's none of my business, to begin with. Second, I'd have to say where she did it. With her being moved, it's going to make my story look strange. But really peculiar. Why would anyone want to move a dead body?"

For a moment there Elsie had thought he was trying to

be protective of John Brown. She asked, "What if I slip up and tell what really happened?"

"You don't know what really happened," Jim said. "You only know what I told you."

"That, at least, is true."

Jim said he was not asking her to lie. "You heard a shot, you went out, you saw the body where it is now. Right?"

"Right, Jim."

"And my story's the same. Simple and straight."

Elsie went towards the kitchen to turn the potatoes off. "Just so long as you don't move her again."

"Trust me."

One minute later Elsie was walking down the lane. Her legs, she was grateful to note, were unsteady. Although she adored feeling competent, she hated to think of herself as lacking heart. She had been glad of those stabs of emotion and knew that if she now allowed herself to dwell on the agony of soul which had brought that young woman to the stage of taking her own life, she would hurt. That was for later, like a fresh consideration of John Brown's story.

Elsie, however, went on to think of what her husband had just come to accept. She had almost forgotten that absurdity, a fairy tale in which some atavistic part of her nevertheless believed. Absurd or no, was there any other explanation for the suicide? If it was one. If Jim hadn't made a mistake. If John Brown hadn't shot the woman. If he and Jim weren't in this together.

Unhappy with these thoughts, Elsie took her mind away. She wondered why so many people, Jim included, were afraid of the police, often manifesting their fear by being cocky, which policemen loved. Coming from a family tradition of nurses and law officers, Elsie knew that the neutralising attitude was meekness; that inside most policemen there was a nasty little boy struggling to stay hidden; that no other job existed which offered so much power while asking for so little in the way of brains and education.

Elsie reached the hardtop, turned left, sharpened her stride. At the same time she realised both that her face had taken on a cast of drama and that she was feeling stimulated. She smiled weakly in embarrassment.

Missy hummed a catchy tune as she gazed up at the dangling hardware, though she was neither feeling musical nor interested in buying. Her pose was to suggest that she knew everything about the new couple in the village but wasn't going to say.

Facing Missy where she stood leaning back against the counter were three customers. Behind her was Marsha, who said repeatedly that they looked pretty ordinary to her, the new couple. Missy hummed on.

She was no more aware of her act than she was of her annoyance. That she knew as little as everyone else about the couple irked her like the continuing needle of John Brown. She was still unsure about his fame, in its truth and its nature, despite having mentioned the Ku Klux Klan around and having hinted to Jim and having made a second fruitless trip above to provoke an outdoor meeting.

Had she considered her mild tension, Missy would have put it down to the fact that she was trying to decide whether or not she should sit on the counter. It needed only a little hoist and was a terrific thing to do. But what if Marsha asked her to get off?

The customers, one man and two women, rising nobodies, went on telling what they had heard they were saying about the new people. Missy exchanged her hum for an amused expression. She moved both hands back to dabble the counter edge. "Ordinary but okay," Marsha said. "And she's kinda sweet."

Everyone looked around as the doorbell rang. In came Elsie Braddock. Missy and Marsha said, "Hi." The customers said, "Hi, Elsie." Giving no answer Elsie approached but stopped short of a normal arrival, as though she were coming for punishment. She said, "Well." It echoed like the last word in an argument.

Marsha asked in a colonel voice, "What's up?"

"I have to use the phone," Elsie said dully, her face bland. "Something terrible's happened."

She had everyone's attention. Offended as an uncalled understudy, Missy raised a hand to caress the twinge of ache in her breastbone.

Elsie said in the same bald manner, "I have to call town for the police and an ambulance."

Everyone nodded her on except Missy, who stroked herself while thinking, I'm screwing your husband.

The man asked, "The police?" Elsie, looking at Marsha, appeared not to have heard. One of the women customers asked, "Police?" Elsie went on looking at Marsha, who asked, "You have to call the police?"

Elsie said, "Yes, there's been an accident."

People asked: Car accident? Somebody fall down? Anyone we know? Shaking the questions off, Elsie began to tell about a woman, a stranger, who had appeared on the top lane.

Her hand sinking, Missy listened in a disgust that grew to surmount her interest, even swamp her pleasure in Elsie's waste of the opportunity, so drab was the teller's delivery, so poor her overall style.

Everyone talked at once, the customers in a hurry to be the first to repeat the news to each other. Marsha went around to the newsbearer, embraced her, and then drew her towards the telephone. No one noticed Missy slip away.

Outside, she strode across the road. Gustav's stoop was deserted. After thrusting inside the bar she paused, swaying, to note that although many of the lunchtime crowd had gone there was still a goodly group.

"Gimme a brandy," Missy called out to Florence as, allowing herself a slight stagger, she went to the bar. "Oh my God."

Over the following hour most everybody in Shank came up to view the body, standing at a distance with their chins raised. Many called on the Braddocks, who at one point had a dozen people in their living room and who told their version of the event over and again. Jim took on the mild swagger of a survivor, Elsie wished she dare cover the woman with a sheet. Indoors and out, everyone left when sirens warned in the distance.

There were three vehicles: police, coroner, ambulance. The skirmish of panic in which they arrived was denied when the occupants alighted with the laziness of boredom. Jim and Elsie withdrew to wait.

They had nothing to say. Jim felt normal if nervous, Elsie felt depressed. They sat neatly with their hands on the table like shy spiritualists, exchanging nods and pulls of mouth at every prominent sound from outside.

The trooper who came in finally called himself Wexon. He was fortyish, handsome, and model-like in his uniform, large. That he was not of lowly rank he made plain by touching insignia here and there, the while glancing at faces to make sure his efforts had been understood.

Standing, he brought out a notebook. "Before we get to details, folks, suppose you just tell me this: between the shot and you-all going outside, would there've been time for someone to fade? A murderer, like."

Elsie and Jim, standing by their chairs, unisoned a negative. As though he had known all along what the answer was going to be, Wexon gave a small, twisted smile. He said, "Details."

That took ten minutes. Jim felt worried by the ease of it all, Elsie felt like a schoolgirl who coaxes correct questions out of the teacher.

Wexon put his notebook away. He stood in a pose which reduced his height by a foot, hips going one way, shoulders the other. The hand of one dangling arm nearly touched his knee.

He said, "So you neither of you saw the deceased until after she was dead, eh?"

Elsie said, "That's right, officer." Jim was tempted to say they had answered that question already three times, but, he told himself, he knew better than to rub cops the wrong way.

"Name of the deceased is Helen Grant, her papers say," Wexon said. "Mean anything to you? Helen Grant?" He looked from one to the other. "Helen Grant?"

"We've never heard of her, officer," Elsie submitted.

"She's from Baltimore way. You folks know anyone up there in Baltimore?"

Jim said, "No. And we've never been there."

Like rising fear, a siren began. Past the window went the ambulance, followed by the coroner's car. Wexon asked, "And you neither of you ever saw the lady before in your lives, that right?"

Jim smiled patiently on. "I think we've already made that quite clear."

The trooper looked at him with heavy, happy eyes. He

said, "I hope this is no incon*ven*ience to you, trying to do right by some poor dead woman and get all the facts."

Jim's smile tightened. "Oh no. You have your job to do."

"Like, for all we know, she could be a friend of yours and you shot her in a fight. We don't know, do we?"

Jim shook his head. Elsie sighed.

"So what we have to do is ask a coupla little questions and hope we don't incon*ven*ience nobody."

"We're not in the least bit put out, officer," Elsie said. "We're only too pleased to do what we can to help, such as walking to the village to call the authorities and keeping people here away from the body."

Still looking at Jim, Wexon said, "When y'all come into the station later today to make your statement, I'll have 'em take your fingerprints."

Elsie said, "That's standard, I imagine."

Wexon told her without looking at her, "You needn't come, ma'am. Just your man here."

Pale, Jim said, "If I'd shot the lady, you don't suppose I'd be stupid enough to leave my fingerprints on the gun, do you?"

"Fella, I don't have no idea what you'd be stupid enough to do. That's why I'm asking questions, see, to find things out."

"Sure sure," Jim said to placate, hating the man and despising himself. "You have your job to do."

"As I believe you already mentioned," Wexon said. While he was changing position, reversing his pose, a knock sounded. The trooper who entered in answer to his superior's call took up a subdued guard on the wall.

"Jobs now," Wexon said. "What d'you work at, fella? Right off the top of my own head I'd suspect you was a artist."

Elsie said they both were. Jim said, "We sell mostly to tourists."

"Make lots of money?"

"A living. We get by."

Of the ceiling Wexon asked, "Regular *married* folks?"

"Very," Elsie said.

Of Jim, Wexon asked, "Smoke dope?"

Elsie said she wouldn't allow it in the house and Jim said, "We don't need stuff like that."

Wexon looked tired. He said, "Let's get to these other people up here."

Min Kuzak dealt with, Jim said, "John Brown's in residence." He winced because it sounded so pompous.

"What's he like?"

"A nice quiet man," Elsie said.

Wexon, of his shoulder, asked: "Anything?"

"One guy said he'd heard he was KKK and a woman said she'd heard he was famous."

"That right, folks?"

Jim said John Brown was definitely not Ku Klux Klan and Elsie said, "He's one of those eccentric billionaires, officer. Knows all the top people but likes to live simply himself, as well as incognito."

Wexon told his shoulder, "With no one knowing where he is." He straightened. "Well, I guess that wraps it for here."

When the policemen had gone Jim asked, "Why'd you say that?" To ease the ache in his legs he sat down.

"Cos I'm a smart cookie," Elsie said.

He doubted if there would be more. Helen of Grant & Teague was the only one with the right connection from that Baltimore stay, in an ideal suburb where everyone wanted to be let alone. It could have lasted years.

She caught him unawares in the backyard—a second sighting. The first, he learned, not having known of it himself, had been when her male partner in real estate had met new client John Walterson at night outside the office, by arrangement. Helen Grant, working late, had watched idly through the Venetians. Two months later, on coming to see if he was satisfied with his rental, she saw him again. She lost herself.

Lying on the chesterfield face down, John hurried his mind onto the next step: mechanics. He had been through it once already but no matter. It kept him from the fact of death, of a life wasted for an emotional aberration.

Helen has a friend in the local bank. With discreet questions involving many clients she finds out about the transfer of John Walterson funds to a John Cartwright in a town in Georgia. Realising from the name-change that there has probably been another change, she asks not by name when she starts to drive around—town, suburbs, villages —but for a man who likes to shun the world. Simple enough.

John was beginning to drift towards recalling the pleading voice when he ran more interference. With gratifying disgust he realised how strong still was his instinct for survival, for protection of self. Even while shattered that Helen Grant had actually done what she had been threatening, even though awash with pity for her as she lay there dead, he was gaspingly intent on moving the body elsewhere, anywhere, so long as it kept him in the clear.

Although the knock was polite, it made John jump, since he knew it had to be the police at last. He got up quickly and let them in.

The interview was short, with the superior officer asking the minimum of questions. John told of being asleep, hearing no shots, knowing nothing until seeing village people out there. He was sorry he couldn't be more helpful. Had the poor woman really shot herself? It sure looked that way, the officer said. He made enigmatic references to wealth, position, underground organizations, and people's little foibles. After another apology for the interruption, he left.

Sorry to see him go, to be alone again with his thoughts, John watched from the window. As the police car went out of sight, Jim appeared from his cabin. He came along at a march. John went eagerly to the door, opened it, and from inside asked, "You want to walk?"

"Sure," Jim said, stern. "It's all clear out. Elsie's lying down."

Together they went up the lane. John stated, "You believe me now."

"I saw it happen. It was outside your door."

"That's right, Jim."

"You moved her."

"I had to. You understand that, surely."

"Yes," Jim said. "And yes, I believe you now."

John started to talk about the incident. It was an ease to be talking. He would have talked about anything, shoes to kings, but he had to keep to the day's events or Jim would think him insane. He ended, "Wexon was no problem."

"We told him you were a rich eccentric."

They left the lane, went upward through the trees. Jim gave the incident his own angle. John, leading, felt increasingly better, as though every stride took him further from captivity. He was less desperate, recognition of which failed to destroy it by bringing guilt for not regretting more strongly having caused the death of an innocent woman. There was a mitigating clause.

John was still leading when they reached his place, the explanation of which he kept light. After nodding all around in a polite show of interest, Jim said forcefully, "Look. This thing of yours. It seems like it's true."

"The Gift. Yes."

"It's more of a curse, as you said."

John stood with his shoulders touching the big rock. "I didn't know it would be every woman. I thought it was the ability to make any woman I chose fall in love with me. Could be there's been a mistake."

"I believe in this," Jim said. "But even so, I don't believe in magic. I can't."

"It might not be magic or supernatural or anything abnormal like that. I've had plenty of time, as well as the impetus, to consider every possibility."

Nodding as though at some inner tune, Jim sat on the smaller of the two piles of flat stones that John had spent a near-contented hour finding and arranging like a table and seat. "Yes?" he said. "What?"

"Well, it could be a kind of mind-control," John said. "A brain power. Employed, of course, without my conscious knowledge. You see what I mean?"

"Sort of."

"Also, again unawarely, I could be using a sort of hypnotism. A primitive sort. The sort that witch-doctors use. It's pretty similar to mind-control."

Jim said he guessed that was possible. "And it wouldn't be supernatural." He looked relieved.

Still peddling old goods John said, "Or it could work the way faith-healing works. My conviction that women will fall in love with me impresses itself on their emotions. It would be like giving them an order."

"Well . . ."

"Or it could even be that I emit the fact that I'm waiting to fall in love myself."

"You've never been in love?"

"No," John said. "But those theories. They're weak alone, individually. What's most likely is that this power is a combination of all or some of them as well as another factor or factors that I haven't found yet."

"Odd," Jim said, "that you've never fallen for anyone."

"I meant not seriously. Lightly, yes. I was always being captivated. Continually so."

"You had a lot of female friends?"

"More than male, yes. I admire women. I respect them tremendously. In the general sense, I love them. I think they're far finer human beings than men."

Jim asked a dozy, "You do?"

"Absolutely," John said. Like a cat and a shin, he rubbed his back against the rock. "They're less cynical, more compassionate. They're far more loyal, more loving, more altruistic, far more protective of life, of anything living. They're altogether more decent." Another rub. "I think women will inherit the earth."

"Well now."

"It's inevitable, as I see it. Their gradual entry into politics will change one of these days, accelerate. They'll become politicians and leaders in hordes, outnumber the men in government service on all levels. The world will change."

"If you think there'll be no more war—"

"There won't," John said.

"Come on. As Elsie says, every woman practically who's gotten into a position of power has been inclined to Fascism."

"That's because she took on masculine attributes while fighting in that masculine world of politics. She had to, to survive, let alone prosper. In the future she'll be able to remain her own feminine self, with so many other women in the political world."

"No more war?"

"Unthinkable," John said, rubbing. "Nor will there be famine, torture, or any of those charmers. There might not even be any more strikes. After all, it's the wives who always suffer most."

"Psychological damage," Jim said. "That's what men suffer, being out of work."

"And the wives have to put up with it, as well as handling the psychological damage of their own."

"Brave New World."

"Or Timid. A world I won't see."

"You're not all that old."

John strolled away from the rock. He said, "I meant I won't see it because, as is almost inevitable, if another woman falls in love with me, just one more, I'm going to do what Helen Grant did. I'm going to take my own life."

"I see."

"I've promised myself. It's final."

"I see," Jim said again. He had started to assume his discomforted look.

Circling, John said, "To get back to the way I feel about women. It's possible that this—let's call it devotion—that it comes across to women and they reciprocate."

"In that case all females, of any age at all, would fall for you."

"I disagree. I think that the animal in me would instinctively project this devotion most powerfully to females of the child-bearing years."

"Well, I don't know," Jim said, getting up.

John said, "So again, perhaps this devotion is added to that combination of possibilities I mentioned to produce the Gift. In theory. In reality, I doubt if it's feasible for a complex combination like that to happen at a snap. Unless it's through the power of suggestion."

"Your own?"

"No, from a man called Paul Ganieri. I'll tell you about him as we walk down."

They left the place. Moving around a tree John said, "Thank you for not telling the police about Helen Grant's change of position." Jim said he could break the law for a friend.

SEVEN

In Shank, the suicide reigned as topic king. Although people had killed themselves before in the village, they had been locals, not mysterious and smartly dressed strangers. Talk proceeded at a low seethe. When Jake Milano returned briefly to collect a forgotten something, he was treated not so much as an unwanted anti-climax, more as an outsider who, boringly, wasn't in the know.

The drama's stars were Missy and Jim. This was due to the fact, well chewed, that, after an initial verbal flow, when they seemed to hint at secret knowledge, even, it was interpreted, at having witnessed the shooting, they became curiously reticent on the subject. That sealed opinion far more successfully than if they had broadcast from the chapel lot. They were courted for news of developments, they were looked at more than anyone else.

Because of her forbidding air in respect of the suicide, Elsie was avoided. Even less heed was paid to the nobody who claimed to be the last person to see the dead woman alive, having helped her when she had asked him where the hermit lived. Nobodies were like that.

The deceased was named as Helen Grant; her car was taken away from where it had been left in the village, the autopsy confirmed death by a bullet in the heart. A score of Shankites attended the inquest in town, including Elsie Braddock but not her husband or Missy, which omission caused interest.

Sole witness of consequence during the twenty-minute hearing was a woman from Baltimore, who said she believed she was Helen Grant's closest friend. Helen had been depressed for months, she said, apparently in connection with her love for a man who would have nothing to do with her. The man was called John Walterson, which meant nothing to anyone. Witness admitted she had never met the man and knew little about him. Without leaving their box the jury returned a verdict of suicide while of unsound mind.

Following his bout of mild euphoria on the afternoon of Helen Grant's death, John, as he had expected, sank into a gloom. He suffered in his isolation, lacking even visits from his neighbour. With pain like that from a lovely nostalgia, in a slough as ugly as broken teeth in a comb, he struggled for recovery. He treated himself like an older brother who was sick.

Whereas the death of an unknown woman in a backwater by any other name would have gone unnoticed by the nearby world, its locale revived interest in Shank, village of oddball artists and peculiar doings. A limerick on the affair was passed around town like a dirty joke. Wags speculated on Shank becoming Suicide Spot of the Southland. More tourists drove out in the lengthening evenings.

Two painters, a sculptor, and a potter set up their regular sales pitches near the village core. Jim set up also, doing double attendance service because Elsie was suffering from migraine. The bar ran out of beer on Saturday night and Store Marsha said that if this extra business kept up she would have to hire an assistant.

Majors at a private supper (Elsie, Jim, and Missy had declined) agreed jokingly that next you knew some company would be moving in to build a motel here. After that there was a long silence, as though someone had questioned the value of freedom. The group of diners did not finish their evening in Gustav's.

A reporter on the town daily, being in need, photographed a prone red rose in the dust of his backyard. The caption that accompanied the published picture stated site to be where Helen Grant had taken her life, donor of the flower unknown. The fad this started stayed minor only because, it was agreed, the photograph appeared in the same edition that headlined a sensational murder. Mere dozens of people over the following days came out to look for the place where they could drop a red rose.

Without conscious intention, Missy and Jim eluded each other as thoroughly as ex-spouses. Missy was noted being pensive at her posing work, in the bar, and when she wandered around the village. Jim was seen to be introspective as he sat at his roadside pitch. Outsiders watched the locals and the locals watched Jim and Missy. Never had their major potential been so powerful.

Gradually, like a trodden blade of grass arising, John recovered. The process took more will than last time. As usual he was aided by knowing that his responsibility wasn't total and by acknowledging anew the possibility that the recent years could be part of a monster's daydream.

At the junction of lane with highway, Elsie stopped. A little way along towards the village, on the road's other side, was the pitch she had chosen as preferable to one in the village when she had been avoiding Philip. Why Jim was using it, and had been doing so for the past week, she didn't know. Might it be that he was avoiding Rachel?

Nor did Elsie know why, ignoring accepted procedure, Jim sat there minus sketch-pad, something else which had become regular. He had hardly worked in weeks, in fact, as Elsie was aware, but only during the past days had he gone into his present phase, gazing inertly at nothing as though trying to will his muse to materialise.

Elsie walked on. While her guilt at letting Jim do all the pitch-minding had been pleasant, she no longer had a reason to invent headaches: the tourists drawn by the suicide had trickled down, the last rose had been picked up from whatever spot its donor had been told by a Shankite was the right one. The affair was finished. So she had no cause to think that in selling pictures she might be profiting by someone's tragic death.

In any case, that additional pleasure, from feeling nicely sensitive, noble, had been dulled by her knowing that sentiment should not have to be paid for by someone else, as though it were an operation.

Elsie arrived at the pitch, where beside Jim squatted a contender couple. The man was rolling a joint, the girl was holding her lighter ready.

Not for the first time, Elsie told herself that the answer to Jim's recent behaviour could be narcotic. As all new arrivals in Shank quickly learned, one sure way to recognition as a living being was to be a good joint-passer.

The couple said, "Hello, Elsie."

"Hi there. Hi, Jim."

"Hi," Jim said, sitting up on the campstool. With eyes that were as clear and fine as one's own advice he looked at Elsie's satchel. "Supper's here."

"No, it's not sandwiches tonight, hon. There's a real nice meal in the oven for you."

"How about that."

"I've neglected my husband long enough," Elsie said. "And I'll spend the evening here on duty. My migraine season seems to be all through."

"Oh?" Jim said absently.

When he had strolled off Elsie sat and took out her pad. She began to make warm-up taps of the crayon on the paper, yet without looking around to choose a plant for sketching. She wasn't here for that.

"Elsie?" the man said.

Although she knew that by declining, even graciously, a smoke, it would be seen as putting the couple in their contender place, Elsie shook her head smilingly at the proffered joint. With things back to normal now, except for the situation with Jim, she wanted to do some thinking.

While Elsie had accepted the suicide as genuine, not murder or accident, that, she knew, did not have to mean that John Brown was in any way involved. He had claimed to be. Or rather, Jim said he had claimed to be, just as he had said the shooting had been outside John's door. Elsie realised indeed that for all she was aware John Brown's story might have nothing to do with John Brown but be a figment of Jim's imagination, including the entry into the drama of a larger-than-life-sounding character called Paul Ganieri.

With a mumbled good-bye, the couple left with their cigarette. Elsie started making doodles in a corner of her sketch-pad. She knew she was skirting the question that she had been too shy to face all along: assuming that the story of love did come from John Brown, not Jim, could it be true?

Elsie skirted again. She recalled the inquest, which she had attended out of some sort of respect—she wasn't sure about that herself—and after which she had condoled with the witness from Baltimore.

But what if Helen Grant *had* killed herself out of love for John Brown?—Elsie tried. Say that was perfectly true, and that yes, the same thing had happened before, it still didn't necessarily mean that all women fell desperately in love with John, only some. Which wasn't all that rare. They did exist, those men and women who had an irresistible charm for certain of their sexual opposites.

Maybe, Elsie thought, it had something to do with astrology. Maybe people who were born on such and such a date at precisely a certain time were inevitably drawn towards those born at another particular moment. Maybe all love was an accident of birth.

Happy with her thinking, Elsie drew long graceful lines on the edge of her sketch-pad and considered genes. If every direct woman forebear, from Mother back, had fallen in love with the same type of man, wouldn't that be inclined to make you feel impelled likewise?

Unshy, Elsie mused that genes and astrology and all those theories which Jim had said he had suggested to John could combine to create the Gift/Curse, in, of course, a fractional way, not as told by the story.

Elsie further mused, after a minute's doodling with hand and mind, that whenever John Brown met for the second time a woman of the right type, he, knowing that she was bound for unhappiness, would be unable to stop himself from expressing the most profound compassion.

With a flourish of wrist, Elsie started to sketch. As model she chose a shriveled brown weed. When she put down pad and crayon it wasn't that the drawing was finished, but because she couldn't wait a moment longer to change the tedious way Jim had arranged the pictures.

Elsie wished she had the sense to ignore superstition and the courage to believe in her reduction of the Gift to a possible but outlandish reality; the guts to call on John Brown, who may be the loneliest man in the world. But she knew she was too sensible to be courageous.

In a while, humming softly as she re-stood the outdoor

show, being particular, Elsie was enjoying pique that Philip hadn't ignored her claim of fidelity.

Jim ate his dinner the way a dog eats caviar. He would have known how it tasted only if it were putrid. His mind was given to what lay ahead, a mission with far-stretching consequences. He was excited.

With his acceptance of the Gift as true, Jim had started trying to find what had proved elusive for John: some way to put the mysterious power to work for positive ends.

As Jim saw the matter, it was as much for the power's owner as for others. John would feel forgiven, reprieved, if he could outnumber the women he had hurt with those he was benefiting.

The first day, fired by pride at being so altruistic, Jim had sunk himself so deeply into thought as to mildly lose contact with the world about him. He failed to produce a solution. Next day was no more fruitful, yet his cogitation, instead of tapering off out of discouragement, became more concentrated than before, rendering him for long slopes of time even less aware of externals. This was because his thinking had turned commercial. He didn't notice the difference.

With the quiet stimulation of the hunter who rises at dawn, as unfamiliar as before with what was going on outside his head, Jim had considered various schemes.

He saw John appearing on television commercials, with women in their multitudes buying whatever he recommended. He saw him as an actor, the highest-paid star in the history of motion pictures, the world's movie houses packed to the doors with females every time a John Brown vehicle was screened. Jim saw his neighbour filling stadiums as a performer of some kind. He saw him receiving vast sums to speak at rallies on behalf of politicians; or larger sums from rivals to not speak. He saw that same reverse working with rival television sponsors. He saw it all in deadly earnest.

Jim had itched to discuss with someone his ideas. But the moment wasn't old enough for him to talk to John himself and Elsie had no concept of business. Missy would have been perfect, except that Jim discovered, not without a splash of surprise, that he was losing interest.

He hadn't been missing her company, for one thing, Jim pointed out. For another thing, it was clear from the way people had been looking at him lately and behaving towards him that he had become a true major. For thing three, he could be on the verge of flying high: the Gift had fantastic potential. In short, he was growing out of Missy.

As the days passed Jim had thought up other schemes to make money, his fervour that of a convict who plans escape. One idea he cared for particularly, since it had its kind side, was of John founding a charity. Half of the donations would go to the founder, which would be fair enough, no one could complain, for the other half wouldn't have existed except for the charisma and leadership of John Brown.

The charity scheme, however, like all the others, had a flaw: there was no part in it for Jim Braddock. Unless, of course, he became some manner of assistant to chief John. That suited Jim like losing an eye. Furthermore, there would still be the danger, as with previous ideas, of John being exposed to women *en masse* and therefore creating widespread, wholesale havoc, which could end in his own self-murder, thus destroying the scheme by its success.

Quietly and craftily Jim had persisted with his cogitations. What he sought now was a plan that would be good to himself and protective for John, the goose.

Jim found that he was in love with the concept of

wealth. Often he was reminded of how the policeman Wexon had treated John through believing him to be a billionaire. He was reminded of everything he had ever coveted and been unable to own, from a lavish home to a fleet of sports cars. He realised he hated macaroni. He was appalled, not cheered, when Elsie clapped her hands because he had sold one of her pictures for thirty dollars, a pathetic thirty dollars. He grew morose, having had the smell of genuine money and not being able to find the source.

Yesterday, early afternoon, Jim had recognised what could be the answer. It came to him at the pitch when he was salestalking a woman who said she was just browsing. She did so without getting out of her new Cadillac.

Patronage. That was absolutely it, Jim had thought in seethy triumph. Jim Braddock, and his wife Elsie, would have a patron of the arts. They would have as much money as they needed for as long as they wanted, supplied by the woman, carefully chosen for her lack of relatives and the extent of her wealth, who would fall in love with John Brown and be enraptured to follow his advice.

His own role Jim saw as being partly that of guardian. He and the security net he would arrange couldn't fail to keep John safe from other females.

Jim pictured the two couples sharing an enormous, beautiful palace somewhere in Europe, maybe Venice. There would be male servants, a garage full of cars. He pictured so fondly that it all became as clear to him as Shank, which now seemed irrelevant, even foolish.

Jim had thought out the idea from every direction, loving it the more on seeing how practical it was in comparison to those early schemes. By today, save on one score, the idea had become so feasible that he almost told Elsie.

But there was that one score to be resolved first. Would John make friends with the idea?

Yes, Jim thought, if it were offered to him slowly, not as the finished plan but by first musing aloud about how great it would be if they could live in beautiful surroundings; John, worry-free, taking life easy with his reading and strolls around a private estate, Jim and Elsie painting seriously in the large studio with its many-paned window bathing them in pure northern light.

Jim had decided to approach John tomorrow with the opening installment of his idea disguised as wishful thinking. That changed when Elsie showed up at the pitch to take over, which Jim saw as a sign. He would start on John today.

His movements terse, his taste-buds asleep, Jim ate on. He was excitedly aware that the future as it concerned wife and self could be in for a momentous revolution, from life-style to artistic development. Jim rode in a gondola, he roughed out the blurb for the catalogue for his first one-man in oils.

After supper Jim washed his dishes, telling himself with wounded eyes that he wasn't such a bad guy. If Elsie was good enough to fix him a real meal, he was good enough to take care of the plates.

He left the house. When he was nearing the last cabin its door opened. John, struggling two chairs out, called that they could sit outdoors. "These evenings are so fine and still."

Jim the guardian asked, "Is that a good idea?"

"We have the approaches covered."

"And you could quickly dodge inside."

"Just so."

As they sat Jim stated, "You're feeling better."

"Have been for a couple of days now," John said. "I haven't seen much of you lately."

After blowing out like a man unburdening himself of a sack of cement, Jim told about working down at the pitch double time. The opportunity he saw only when he had stopped feeling apologetic.

He said, "You have no idea how tough it is, being an artist in my situation."

"I do, as a matter of fact, Jim. I knew lots of painters in Paris."

"I bet they had terrific studios, eh?"

"And talking of Paris," John said. "I wanted to tell you about Paul Ganieri."

Jim said fast, "You already did."

"Not all of it. Only about the man himself. I didn't tell you the important thing."

Grudgingly: "What's that?"

"How I came to get the Gift."

There was no hurry about Venice, Jim thought, receding. He said, "I thought it just happened."

"No, I earned it. How about a beer?"

"Wasting time is a luxury only the young can afford," John said as he sat again. Like an abstaining voter, he felt comfortable in his mind. He was glad he had been able to steer their talk in the desired direction. "I was heading for forty." He smiled. "Which is old until you get to be fifty."

Jim opened his beer. "Earned it?"

"So, feeling the pinch of years, there was a now-or-never essence about the whole affair for me, apart from any other consideration."

"You got the Gift through that Ganieri?"

"Right, Jim."

"What were his terms?"

"I'll come to that," John said. He sipped from his can.

Jim said, "And if you got it from him, you should be able to give it back. Or he should be able to take it away." He had a hurried drink.

"I'll come to that as well. First I want to try to make you understand why I went through with it."

"That's no problem."

"It might be when you hear what I had to do in exchange for the Gift."

"Yeah?"

John looked away, scanned trees, said, "I had to kill someone." Still feeling comfortable he turned back. "That's what I had to do."

Jim was intent, it seemed, on scratching a spot of grease on the thigh of his jeans. He asked, "Is that honestly true? Honestly? No crap?"

"It is, Jim. You have my word."

Scratching: "Well, Jesus, John."

"A man will do a lot to gain perfection."

"Even so."

"I'm not trying to excuse the fact that I took a human life," John said. He deliberately gave his words a shade more emotion than he was feeling. "I couldn't if I wanted. I'm hoping to show the high degree of temptation."

Jim left his thigh alone, looked up. "I suppose you killed an enemy of Ganieri's."

"I have no idea. That side of the business is a different matter. All Paul would say was that the victim, completely unknown to me, was an unhappy person. Ill with misery is how he phrased it."

"Even so," Jim said again.

"Yes, even so," John agreed. "But see it this way. I was being offered something that I'd craved all my life. From childhood. From realising that my parents were more interested in their hardware store than in me. I wanted love."

"Well yes, I can see that."

"Most people find it at least once—love. I never had. Never. Neither familial nor romantic. I wanted it badly. And the possibility was growing more remote. At least, I felt it was. You understand?"

"Of course, John."

John asked, "What wouldn't a singer do, one who'd been on the bottom rung for twenty years, in exchange for the guarantee of total success?"

"Thousands have killed for less," Jim said, setting his beer on the ground. Upright, he nodded. "Don't doubt it, John. But thousands."

"How I changed from being initially repelled by the idea, onto agreement, I no longer remember. It must've been slow. I do know there were many factors involved, minor ones compared to my need for love, but no less important. For example, there was the matter of belief."

Jim spread flat hands. "You didn't know for sure that the Gift was true."

"Could be I was simply being used as a killer," John said on a nod. "Paid not with money but the promise of a wish come true. But that was one of the negative factors, urging me to refuse. Urging me to agreement was the possibility that the whole thing was some sort of elaborate game. Or a trick. Or it could be that I was undergoing a test for some reason."

"The possibility that there wouldn't really be anyone to kill, once you'd agreed?"

"No, that if I went through with it the supposed victim wouldn't die or even be wounded."

"A set-up."

"Exactly that," John said. "For, as I say, a game or a trick or a test. Though the why of it escaped me."

Jim said he would give it some thought and John went on, "There was my age as well, in a different respect. Most of the people I'd known in Paris, they'd moved on elsewhere or gone back home or they'd settled into marriage. There was a whole new group of young Americans around. They looked on me as an older man."

"You were ready to leave."

"I hadn't thought of it until the Ganieri thing came up, then yes, I realised, or kidded myself I did, that my Paris days were over and done."

"It might've been different if you'd been a painter. Even a poor one."

John said, "Let me put my agreement another way. It's one of the factors. Owning the Gift was outrageously attractive, yes, unquestionably, but I found equally strong the bleakness of a future without it. My future hadn't looked at all bad before, pre-Ganieri, but it looked that way now."

"I can see that all right," Jim said. "Sure."

"Thank you."

"Christ, yes, you must've been tempted. I mean look, who wouldn't be?"

"Would you have been, Jim?"

"Any man would. Or any woman, come to that."

"I don't think so," John said. "Not women."

Jim used his fast manner for "So you agreed."

"In the end. Being so tempted had made me feel terrible. Guilty. I felt much better as soon as I'd made up my mind to go ahead. There is, I know, a certain wriggly pleasure to be gained from being corrupt."

"That right?"

With a sway of finality John said, "Anyway, that's what I

wanted to tell you. About me taking a life." He made his look at Jim a challenge. "You're sitting here with a killer." He looked on. "What do you think of that?"

Jim leaned forward, cleared his throat. Like a forgiven culprit he served a series of unfinished sentences, each chopped off when, it seemed, a better one occurred to him in his attempt to express himself. John sympathised. For his own sake, he felt glad. There was little of condemnation in Jim's aura. John interfered:

"It was an exciting time, I have to admit, once the arrangement was made. My life took on a special, fast tone. But I slept like a child. There was something juvenile about it altogether. Ahead lay trick or treat, and I didn't know which I was hoping for."

John sipped his beer. Jim was sitting up and back, his arms folded, nodding. "Yes," he said.

"A speedy, active time," John said. "I had to prepare to move out of my apartment, arrange a flight to the States. There was a lot to do. I hadn't been so busy in years. I told people there was a family crisis back home. I said I hated to leave."

A sensation which he recognised came over John like a cool realisation. It was a warning: don't give away any more than you need to.

He said, "But let's leave the past. New subject. I just wanted to tell you."

It was getting along for midnight. Gustav's stoop, as it tended to be at this time, was full of people. Mostly majors and upper contenders, they leaned, glass in hand, on wall or rail, or sat on furniture as rickety as Victorian urchins.

Midnight on the bar stoop was a local tradition. Long ago, a poet who was hogging a discussion on the witching hour observed that midnight was with us always. No matter what hour it was, somewhere in the world it was midnight.

Shankites thought about it. They saw those places that were having their midnights as mystical, near to mythical, oases fondling that magic time, that apprentice New Year's Eve, while other peoples were bearing their grim 4 A.M.'s and their horrific five in the afternoons. Shankites thought, and realised of course, that to the sensitive of the elsewhere world Shank had its turn once a day at being dwelled on as wondrous and magical.

Since then, even in bitter weather, the day's last hour would see two or more Shankites sidling onto the stoop. Or so locals assured each other in those interminable talks on Shank lore.

There was a non-romantic aspect to the tradition. It was a place and time of social, economic, political significance, used for announcements and denials and denouements. Then, Marsha broke the news of having bought the store; belligerents met to settle their differences; Penelope Parsons celebrated having won her first acting job; May and Jake Milano swore publicly to love each other forever. The midnight stoop was Shank's pulpit, noticeboard, and proscenium arch.

Like a docker who stops in at the corner bar on his way home Friday night, Elsie's presence was accidental. She had nearly been surprised to find herself here.

After staying late in Marsha's quarters behind the store, gabbing, Elsie had come out onto the hardtop at this point instead of farther along. Seeing that Philip was not on the stoop but that Jim and Rachel separately were, she had developed a craving for gin and tonic.

Sitting near the wall (a nobody, as expected, had given up his seat so he could mention it), Elsie tinkled the ice merrily in her drink and related. She liked being in company, getting a people fix. She didn't need to talk or even listen.

Presently, Jim waved for her attention. Elsie nodded, learned from signals that her husband was going home, watched him leave wearing the same pensive expression that he had worn ever since his visit to John Brown today.

Or, Elsie amended, the visit he had said he had made, just as now he had said he was going home.

Looking around, Elsie noted that Rachel hadn't left. She was sharing a chair with the husband of that new couple in town, talking to him with no more than two inches separating their faces.

This gave Elsie such a confusion of emotions that she turned to the major beside her with a blurted appreciation of his latest sculptures. With a quick suck of breath, startled, he drew back. Reassuringly Elsie grabbed him at bicep and thigh.

When next she looked around it was because of a mild commotion by the front step, the place some people called upstage. Missy stood there. The model was flapping her shawl as if it were a crumb-laden tablecloth. It was as good a way as any, Elsie supposed, to get yourself noticed.

The high grumble of talk lessened but slightly when Missy, shawl still, began to send her gaze around the assembly while calling out a now-hear-this. Her eyes passed Elsie, came back, paused, went on. She stopped calling out.

Elsie told herself she must work harder at remembering to put flowers in her ears. People felt insecure when they saw them missing.

But that, Elsie was sure, was not the reason why the model, without another word, put the shawl over her head, stepped off the stoop, and walked off into darkness.

More likely it was because Jennifer had just come out of the bar.

A small glass inside her hand, Jennifer moved onto the vacated upstage, leaned against a support post, and swung slowly to face the gathering. Talk took a swooping drop—and quite rightly, Elsie mused.

This was Jennifer, who had figured in most of the famous drinking scenes that were talked about at three in the morning by majors who were failing to create a famous drinking scene. The Jennifer who had had seven abortions and was one of Gustav's many owners, having sold out after her first attack of delirium tremens. Jennifer, who, piss drunk, had been arrested in New York for stealing a policeman's horse, in New Orleans for bending a jazz-club musician's trombone, in San Francisco for daubing "Desire" on the side of a streetcar. The Jennifer who had lured to her bed in Shank three famous writers and a senator, who had been asked to leave every bar in town, and who had dropped more acid, it was said, than some mothers drop their children's names.

Jennifer stood there in a jaunty pose, no longer slim but skinny, no longer bonny but spent. Each of her fifty years showing its eighteen months on her face, she stood there as if she thought she was just a crazy, young, attractive, passionate, infuriating, wild, forgivable kid. Elsie smiled softly. Had it not been for her secret lake, she would have wept.

Until, concentrating, she began to get the gist of what Jennifer was saying in her languorous way and with her pugilist rasp of a voice. As she would be moving permanently to town soon in order to be on hand for her Alcoholics Anonymous meetings, Jennifer wanted it known that her cabin was available at the old low rent.

EIGHT

If she had not had the impression that John Brown was a secret celebrity, Missy might not have been so profoundly affected by the suicide of an unknown woman. Tired of living in a state of aggravation over being kept in the twilight, her emotions flung themselves at the tragedy like a slum family greeting money.

This was after Missy's role of newsbearer in the bar, after she had gone with others up to see the body, and after she had returned home to fix supper. With no preface, the fact of death now securely digested, she realised of a sharp, sudden like a rap on the head that a life had been terminated. She was moved and shocked.

The author of the crime occupied her for a while. But she put that aside when she began to get foolishly fanciful, link Ms. Grant and John Brown together: she, a fan of his, comes to lay herself at his feet, and when he spurns her she shoots herself. Sometimes, Missy was glad no one could read her silly mind.

What took over Missy's thinking was female-youthful-dead. The trio haunted her like a hated chore still undone over the following days, and, bearing various disguises, sneaked into her nightmares. She too was female and youthful. She too could die.

Life, Missy reasoned, was short. It was also what you made it. You were only young once and there were no laughs in the graveyard and you should never put off till tomorrow what you could do today.

Missy wanted it all to happen at once, in her here and now prime time. The long-term future had become as interesting and appealing to her as dark bags under the eyes.

What Missy wanted to start with was to be officially accepted by all as Jim Braddock's mistress; his woman, his support, and his inspiration. That was the trio which began to take over from the other, gloom to glitter, while Missy went about locked in thought like a doggerelist with delusions of grandeur.

Although she was aware of being paid a generous measure of attention, and aware that it was because everyone now knew about herself and Jim, that was not enough. Pre-suicide it would have been; not post.

That was why ten days after the death of Helen Grant, Missy went into the store. It was her fourth visit of the afternoon. Jim, she had gathered, would be dropping in to return a cooking gadget which his wife had borrowed from Marsha and would, she knew, linger to talk and drink a root beer. Earlier, he had been absent. Now, no.

With the bell above her chittering like the applause of tin soldiers Missy paused to look over, return the glances of, some dozen people, including Jim and the two majors he was drinking pop with at the dispenser.

Missy was reminded of Gustav's stoop last night when, lush on 'shine, she had been on the verge of announcing her affair with Jim. What had stopped her was seeing Elsie there. Missy prided herself on her subtlety.

She was conscious of the waxing attention, for which she held a gloat, as she went forward from the door. Seeing the approach, Jim faded out his talk to watch.

Missy, underplaying the scene, kept her saunter staid in

heading for the dispenser, rounding goods with a kind smile for their sad lack of life, shimmering past customers as though afraid that shopping might be infectious.

She came to a stop at Jim's side. He gave a wary grin. His eyes flicked about as if looking for somewhere to hide. At a deliberate pace, Missy reached up and gave him a small pat on top of his head.

Arm lowered again she said in a true whisper, "Come down to my place in five minutes. It's urgent."

She left before he could answer. Back near the threshold she called out a general farewell and, tense, blew around kisses in the forefinger-tip style of the top majors. It was the first time she had ever used it. Her daring put a clamp on her lungs. She hurried out.

Down at her cabin Missy drew the drapes, lit a pair of candles. Next she undressed, taking off garments until she wore only her T-shirt, which she intended keeping on because of a chill in the air.

But alone, her T-shirt was non-alluring, Missy decided, looking down to pluck at the material with the dismay of someone who discovers he's wearing dung. She savaged it off and got another. It was smaller. It was so much smaller that she only just managed to get it on.

When Missy had stopped chuckling shakily at herself for that bit of panic there when she couldn't get her head through, she took stock. The shrunken garment held her breasts tight, which she found pleasant, and the shortness showed her navel, which gave her an unexpected erotic charge. This she heightened by putting on the five-inch-heel shoes she had never been able to wear in public Shank. Body taut all over, spread from the core tautness of her bottom, she stalked out the room like a warrior with ten scalps. Vaguely, she felt famous.

Jim came. As always, he entered with the cocky stealth

of a suspicious husband. Missy was at hand. They embraced. Between flamboyant kisses they agreed that they hadn't seen much of one another lately. It was one of those things, Jim offered.

"There was that suicide, too," Missy said, easing back. "Everyone was upset."

"And I've been busy with the pitch."

Missy eased further back and began to unbutton Jim's shirt. "With not much help from that wife of yours, until recently."

Jim raised his eyebrows in the middle. "That's true."

Shirt off, Missy took it to a chair, which enabled her, in doing a folding, to bend over thoroughly. She went back, slapped Jim's hands away from his belt, herself opened his jeans, and shucked them down. Her brow she rested on his breastbone as a balance for him as he stepped free. She could hear him holding his breath to keep his belly in.

They went to the bed and fell onto it in a gaspy tangle. Jim was rabbit-quick. Rather than be irked, Missy was given a cozy feeling of superiority as well as the impetus to continue with her ultimatum. Damply extricating herself, she went to her clothes.

She said, "By the way, I have to tell you something."

"Yes, the something urgent," Jim panted.

"No. That was me. I was urgent for you."

"Good deal."

Looking at Jim, who lay in an untidy sprawl as if deboned, she said, "Jim. Listen to me."

"I'm listening."

"I love you, Jim. I want it known that I do and I want it known that I'm your girl friend."

"Sure sure sure."

"Everyone has to know, Jim."

"I guess everyone does know."

"Not Elsie. So she has to be told."

Jim sat up fast enough to make Missy jerk midway into a cringe. But he stayed on the bed, sitting tall with both hands in his lap. He said stonily, "I didn't hear you."

"Yes you did," Missy said, dressing. "Elsie has to be told about us, Jim."

"What're you talking about?"

"It was the suicide of Helen Grant that did it."

His face twisted up at one side Jim asked, "Did what?"

"That lady's tragic demise taught me that I have to be true to myself," Missy said, quoting from a high school play she once auditioned for. "Therefore it follows that I have to be true unto others."

"This is crazy. Nuts."

"My mind's made up, Jim. I'm tired of living a lie. Sorry. Your wife has to be told. If you don't tell her, I will."

Jim launched into dissuasion. He frowned and grinned, laughing with stark eyes whenever Missy repeated her sole argument, that death could happen anytime. Jim's face became as red and shiny as a furious brat's.

Dressed, Missy moved to the door.

Jim asked a shrill "Where you going?"

"Not to see Elsie, sweetheart. Not yet. Maybe not at all. That's up to you. But you can do it, I know. All you need is a day or two to get her prepared for the news, though she must know it already."

Jim said harshly that she didn't. "Not at all. Listen. This is out. Negative. Forget it."

Opening the door Missy said, "I'm going to the store. Come on up when you're ready. I'll buy you a root beer."

"Missy?"

In a casual way he was familiar with the district, whose tenements mainly housed foreign workers—Turkish,

Spanish, Algerian. The ambience of mystery and danger was, he knew, mostly an illusion, one built up of alien smells, tongues, dress, and features from a foundation of the viewer's own thirst for the exotic.

You will be unknown there, Paul Ganieri had said. *In any case, there is the time element.*

The streets were narrow, unclean, stuffed with parked cars, and lit with the majesty of a miser's candle. Up to midnight, they were alive with people and business; after, as quiet as a middle-class funeral.

Safety of movement is almost guaranteed. By two o'clock in the morning, those still out and about will be intent on minding their own dubious affairs.

John wished he could be sure of that. He slowed to a stop on a corner in order to light a cigarette. This corner was the last. He rounded it while lighting up and then stopped again. His hands were steady.

You will be calm, I think. I doubt if you're the type to get an attack of nerves.

At the moment, John's strongest emotion was a light embarrassment at appearing so theatrical: hat pulled low, topcoat collar turned up, he was a movie gangster on his way to a hit. The cigarette he found too much. After another drag he threw it away and pocketed his hand. He touched the gun.

That catch is the safety. Now it's down. Up means ready for action. Nothing could be simpler. You lift the catch, you aim the gun, you pull the trigger.

His tension a crackle like saliva in the ear, John walked on. He had two minutes to go in this the longest day of his life. His general feeling was one of anticipation: near was relief, an end to the waiting. His eyes were alert to the scene.

Parked cars stood opposite closed and dark stores on

rue de la Buanderie. Above, a meagre spotting of lights told of windows. The two people in sight, walking slowly, made no sound to disturb the silence.

It does not, as guns go, make a lot of noise. Not much more than a car's backfire.

One of the pair of walkers, on this side, a man with the rod-straight mien of the overdrunk, he came steadily on. His gaze was down, a stare, as he seemed to be proceeding with the task of fitting his way's straightness with the weave of his mind.

Across the street, a moving bust above cars, the other man was also heading this way. He wore a uniform cap. He was almost at the doorway which John had already established.

It used to be a milliner's but for a year it's been closed. The entrance is recessed by a metre or so. That's where your person will be waiting.

John halted again, by a car, acting as though it were his, acting a search for keys. He was telling himself: A game. It's all a game. Not a thing to worry about.

The rigid drunk went by behind, passing close enough for the squeal of air in his nose to be loud. Seconds later, the other man passed the ex-milliner's, which stood half-way along the street.

The person must be there already, John thought. He circled the car to the road, where he held at a growing noise. It brought a fast taxi. In the reborn quiet John walked on beside the cars with his eyes trying to penetrate the doorway's darkness.

There is no question of personal contact, of course. You won't even be able to see him properly, this stranger. To you, he will only be a face in the dark.

John glanced around. The drunk had gone and the man in the uniform cap was going, at the corner. He was no longer in sight when John looked again, before looking back directly at the doorway, which was nearly level. Within it, he could make out a dim form. It stayed dim as he went by.

Almost like shooting at nothing. Stand six feet away and aim for where the chest would be.

Crossing the road on a slant, John edged between cars to the sidewalk. He felt little more than a dull impatience, as though waiting out the national anthem. He had no need to urge himself on or to insist that it was a game.

You will be making a miserable soul peaceful. Please bear that in mind.

Slowly, John walked towards the ex-milliner's. He was at the suggested distance when he stopped opposite the doorway. The form inside, average height, was a length of darkness topped by a smudge of pale.

He will only be a face in the dark.

While bringing out the gun John looked around. The street still lay in drab peace. From beyond came the sound of casual traffic, like kittens fighting.

You are going to become a better man.

John looked back at the suggestion of face. He didn't know if he could truly see movement or merely sense it, the way he was sensing the tension. By touch, as per practice, he moved the safety catch up.

You will perform an act of humanity.

John held the gun forward. He pointed it at the bulk some two feet below the brow. Just as he was realising that, game or test or whatever, he was not going to go through with this, he squeezed the trigger.

Everything was a shock: the upjerk of his arm, the shot's mad loudness, the cry he heard himself give, the way the stranger was flung back to crash against the door.

Shaking, his mouth open, John stepped backwards. His

hips touched a car. In addition to the echoing gunshot he could hear a slamming from his heart. He was terrified. Making a wild swing around he began to run. He saw the gun in his hand but not for any reward would he have stopped in order to put it away. He ran like a fool.

"Did you do it yet?"

"Listen, Missy."

"Maybe you're planning to do it later."

"Maybe I think it would be best for Elsie not to know."

"In that case, Jim, I'll have to tell her myself."

"Actually, I plan to do it tomorrow."

"That'll make it three days. But who's splitting hairs?"

Because Missy had raised her voice, Jim glanced around furtively from where he stood above her table in Gustav's. None of the late-afternoon customers present were paying more than indifferent attention.

His voice lower to encourage impersonation, Jim said, "Meanwhile there's this John Brown thing."

"What's wrong with John Brown?"

"Nothing. He wants to meet you."

Missy gave one long blink. In a more confidential tone she asked, "Me? He wants to meet me?"

Jim nodded. "Today."

"Well, how about that."

"Properly. Not like that other screw-up. It'll be different this time. If you're interested, that is."

"I should just think I am," Missy said, looking pink in pleasure, a tot with a present. "Maybe I'm finally going to hear what he's famous for."

Jim didn't know what she meant by that. He said, "I have to get back to the pitch. Shall we say in an hour? About seven? Behind here on the short-cut?"

"Why can't we meet here?"

"Seven o'clock," Jim said as though he hadn't heard. Leaving on a nod he went out and headed along the road. He was tense but satisfied.

For Jim to decide on counteraction had taken mere minutes: had indeed been there from the moment Missy had delivered her mad ultimatum. Those minutes, later, had been to consciously recognise that he didn't want to, couldn't stand to, refused to, lose Elsie. Which is what surely would happen if she learned of the affair. Which meant that he had to ensure Missy's silence.

How that was to be done had pushed Venice onto a high shelf, where it would keep cool and dry, safe, until the time was right to bring it down again.

Jim had concentrated hard in his search for a solution to the fatuous dilemma. It was a joyless endeavour. Working to hold a marriage together is like slaving on an old house to maintain it in the same state of acceptable decay. Jim considered all possibilities, starting with the most violent and moving to the most bland, homicide to bribery. All were impossible.

Since the girl, without question, was desperately in love with him, Jim knew, the problem had to be resolved quickly. He scratched his head, punched his ribs. He began to suspect that he might get desperate.

The solution that came to Jim in the night's core as he paced the main room on tip-toe was drastic. It was so much so that he rejected it at once, yet drew it back cautiously as if it were a wily trout on his line when he realised that it might be the only chance. He examined the idea. It stayed drastic. Telling himself, however, that he was no defeatist, Jim continued his examination.

It took him until the afternoon to think down from drastic to sensible his solution, which was to end Missy's love for him by having her fall in love with John Brown.

As Jim had never believed even briefly John's story of having shot someone, it was easy for him to come to the conclusion that John hadn't meant it when he talked suicide; when he said that if one more woman fell for him he would kill himself. There was no worry about that. The solution had seemed drastic (wasn't everything dark in the night?) because it could have an adverse effect on patronage plans. For one thing, John, rather than suffer Missy's pestering, might leave the village before agreement had been reached. That, Jim had seen eventually, as he had seen in true focus all other facets of the case, would be fine. He and Elsie would go along.

His mind on that high shelf, Jim returned to his roadside pitch. Kind, he loitered for a while before indicating to the minder nobody that he would like his stool back.

Once today already Jim had been to John's. He went to arrange a special knock, claiming one was necessary so that John would know immediately who was calling, not be made nervous, not need to verify. Six rapid taps followed after a pause by a single fist-edge thud, that's what they agreed on, as well as the fact that Jim would go only to the back door.

At seven o'clock precisely by the nobody's watch Jim again left him in charge. Closer to the village he went behind cabins and around vehicles to the short-cut's first flight of steps. He sat there to wait.

When Missy appeared, but minutes late, Jim had a band of frustration, being cut off in the middle of a warming sneer at female tardiness. He felt better on reminding himself that, as Missy was insane about him, it wasn't likely she would keep him waiting long. Even better he felt on recalling John's foolish talk of women being better than men, ruling the world.

Jim said, "Let's go."

"Hi, folks."

Jim had turned before the words were dead. Accusingly he said, "Rachel."

Missy asked, "Were you looking for me?"

She stopped nearby. "Just wondered where you guys were going."

Jim began to explain about their hurry and this private business matter. He fumbled off like an actor drying up on seeing that Missy and Rachel were already into a conversation. It was about clothes. Whistling, he began to flick out one leg at the knee. He heard about somebody's knitting, a contender's hat, and the new craze for half-length T-shirts. He thought it curious that despite all that reading John wasn't more intelligent.

It was when he started to feel like a husband that Jim made a move. Using the clipped phrases of emergency he got the women separated and Rachel on her way. He started up the steps with "Let's not waste any more time."

Following, Missy said, "I went home and took a shower. I want to look nice. Is there going to be others there? Don't go so fast. I don't know why we couldn't go round by the road."

Jim lifted one eyebrow: and risk being seen by Elsie? He said, "Time's short."

"But what's happening?"

"Private deal. I want to surprise old John. So I'll tell you what we're going to do."

She was to wait at the side of the door, Jim instructed, as she had done that time with Marsha. Now, when John opened up, she wasn't to make a move until Jim had gone inside; then she could follow and close the door.

"It's a surprise for old John, see."

"Sure," Missy said breathlessly. She was falling back. "Great."

Jim imagined he would have no difficulty in diverting John's attention from the doorway. Once Missy was securely inside, it would be even easier. He would stride through to the front door and leave, the while talking loudly about something he had just remembered he had to do, at once, right now, be back.

Later, Jim planned to claim he hadn't known that the woman was there. Missy would claim otherwise, of course, but John would certainly believe his friend rather than a stranger.

Stumping like a lame goat up the penultimate flight, Jim again got that stupid, maddening niggle of guilt about taking a female for the vital second meeting. He defended as before, by hissing a tune through his teeth and asking what was one female more when there were so many already.

With Missy still on the one behind, Jim went towards the final rise of steps. When he heard voices above he hurried on in annoyance, halting as soon as the voices became clear. His heart then also came to a halt, it seemed. He could feel a silence inside him.

Looking around, all around, as if to demonstrate his smile of disbelief, Jim saw a blond head jerking up into view. He spurted that way, starting off from a racing crouch. "Go back," he said, a whisper. "Change of plans."

Nothing other than those two phrases, repeated, did Jim offer to Missy in her panting bewilderment until he had cajoled her midway back down the short-cut. He left her with, "Don't worry. It's all right. Everything's fine." He was addressing himself.

When he got back to the hearing place they were still talking above, Elsie and John. It made the hairs in his armpits and crotch prickle like stabs from dainty pins.

The speakers' words were unclear but Elsie's voice had a softness which he had never heard before.

Jim put the fingers of both hands in his mouth while sinking to the ground, where he lay on his side, eyes still, listening dreamily to the voices.

Although the evening light was fading, Elsie sat on outdoors, on a log at the end of the cabin. She liked the quality of calm, for one thing, mainly because, having accepted the imponderable, she didn't feel remiss in not trying to fathom its mystical essence.

For another thing, she had nearly forgotten the charm of this view: sky, peaks, flora, and the downwinding road up which presently would come Jim from the pitch. For an important last thing, she found it so refreshing to be able to enjoy a day's end instead of feeling poignant, sympathetic, poor day.

As had happened before recently, Elsie told herself she had no right to feel so happy. And as always, the teller self was as strict with the told as a girl with her doll.

At any rate, Elsie mused in whimsical petulance, if she couldn't stop feeling a glow of contentment, couldn't hold off those thoughts that came with the sweetness of smiles from old lovers, then the least she could do was have the decency to feel guilty.

She could not. She had tried. Several times a day she had looked in mirrors. Nothing.

Just as logic could never brighten Elsie's mood when she was low—though counting blessings at night often helped put her to sleep—so did logic fail to make her emotions behave in what it saw as a respectable manner.

This too formed a refreshing change for Elsie, like her ability to smile at the day's dying. Usually it was the other way around. Usually it was her emotional side who despaired, flapping melodramatic arms at the Elsie who listened to the score instead of empathising with the music, or who dissected the camera angles rather than let the movie be reality.

In any case it was not her fault, Elsie mused with a ripple of smugness. She hadn't done anything. She had merely accepted, given in to the inevitable. So there was no guilt, neither for the concealment nor for that which made it desirable—at least for the present. It would all be out in the open one of these days.

Elsie hummed and tapped her toes. It amused her that she couldn't even feel sad that her beautiful macho pine had fallen. But then, that was matched with the glad over Jennifer.

Elsie's toes tapped on with their message, giving her secret to nature. For two pins or a thumbtack she would have danced. What kept her from that was the thought of Jim catching her at it. He might wonder. He might suspect. All he need do was look at her in a certain way and she was, she knew, liable to blurt the whole thing out and astonish them both. She was like that.

A pie, Elsie decided out of nowhere, slapping both knees to encourage herself in getting up from the log. Her urge to be active she would pamper by baking a pie, pumpkin because John had said that was his favorite.

As Elsie was remembering with indifference that her husband's favorite was banana cream, Jim himself appeared in the distance. With his head lowered and a bundle of pictures dangling from either hand, he came on at a trudge.

Elsie felt a tightening of her throat. Poor Jim, she thought. Dear Jim. Quickly she went forward, to meet and to help. Not for the first time in her life, Elsie wished she understood women.

With most of his flight from the doorway a fuzzy memory, though he could tell by his placid lungs that he had stopped running at some early point, John strode out the final yards. The pension, home for the past few days, beckoned a welcome with its austere lights.

Relieved though he felt to have gotten this far, John tensed up for the possibility of danger. Not only could the night-concierge be on duty instead of stealing a sleep, but it wasn't so late that one of the prostitutes who used the pension couldn't appear with a client, below or above. Either or all could afterwards find suspicious the new transient's nighttime outing and relate it to certain events.

John opened and closed the glass front door with care. The smell of shoes and onion soup took on more tang as he went along the hallway to where it opened out at the stairfoot. He had the caution of a cripple on slime.

Seeing the concierge behind her counter, John first shivered his shoulders and next smiled, both acts involuntary. The woman was asleep in a chair with a section of knitting over her face, the needles angling out from the base like chopsticks. John went by and started up the stairs.

It was in turning onto his floor that he realised that, of course, he still had the gun. Hearing a noise, alarmed falsely, made him slap a hand to the pocket where he must have shoved the gun at some stage.

The moment he was inside his room John put the weapon in a drawer, telling himself not to fret, everything would be okay now until he took off for New York in three days' time. But had it, after all, been wise to delay the flight so as not to rouse suspicion? But how could there be any suspicion, any connection between himself, a respectable American citizen, and some man shot dead in a sleazy district of Paris?

Knowing better than to try to sleep, so replete was he with excitement and fear, John, shoes off, moved around the room. He backed and forthed. Sometimes he formed a circle by rolling across the bed. Once he crawled under it and wondered: is this where I go mad? Or was I mad before? He didn't crawl under the bed again.

When he wasn't briefly thinking about his luck—quiet streets, unseeing concierge—he was dwelling at tedious length on what could be bad mistakes—coming straight here instead of indirectly, not having stopped to get rid of the gun, delaying that flight home.

As the hours passed at the speed of dark, as John despaired of the arrival of noon, when he could go out to get the first edition of the evening newspaper, the fact of his possessing the murder weapon became the principal worry. Finally, it was an ogre.

Once the ogre had John backed into a corner of the room, crouched down like a starveling in the snow, which he didn't know about until he found himself there, his mind having just dissolved the scene of arrest.

The ogre grew. Gorging itself on possibilities like any other neurotic, it grew until John realised that if he didn't soon get rid of the gun he could, being a gibber of nerves, give himself away by doing something rash.

It was first light when he left his room, gun pocketed. The building creaked through the silence. John went downstairs boldly and thrust into view of the desk. It was deserted. He went out.

The hunch John adopted in heading fast for the river made him the same as others who were so early and gauntly abroad in the grey chill. He chose the river as burial ground because that was where criminals always seemed to get rid of their incriminating weapons.

Which presently, while John was using it again to convince himself that this one-mile journey was sensible, brought the recollection that newspapers sometimes told of guns being recovered from bodies of water. The question became: could the gun be traced to Paul Ganieri?

John was poked to a halt by the new worry. It was not for the man who had steered him into this adventure, but for himself. If the gun were found and traced to Paul, Paul might tell the rest of the story.

John changed direction. His new worry he let take over from the one of being caught by the police in possession of the murder weapon, since it concerned a more remote future, was less harrowing.

John furthermore appreciated having a longer journey to make, which he intended continuing on foot: a taxicab driver could afterwards recall his tense early fare.

Paul Ganieri had said he would be leaving Paris, probably. John hadn't forgotten that, but ignored it the way he was ignoring what he suspected to be the true reason for his coming call. Perhaps now, post-event, he would learn if he had been involved in some kind of game, innocent or otherwise.

A police car crawling an approach sent John into an alley. On emerging, he wore his trouser cuffs turned up like a deliveryman and on his shoulder carried an empty carton.

The box he discarded beside a pile of garbage bags within sight of Paul Ganieri's house. He hurried onto the door. His knocking was futile, bringing only the glance of a passing woman.

John circled to the rear, where he knocked once, as a

gesture, before investigating the backgarden's toolshed. He came out with a spade.

The spot he chose was right beside the house. He could neither be seen by neighbours nor by anyone beyond the garden wall. A cat bore witness to his slow, quiet digging, his interment two feet down of the wiped gun, his correcting of the surface.

Ogre dead, John put back the spade, making sure its handle was as clean as the weapon, being fussy. The shed's dirt floor looked up at him with the appeal of turf. Abruptly, he knew exhaustion. He lay down with a rolled sack for his head and at once swooped away into a princely sleep.

It had taken Jim until his return home from the pitch to absorb in full, completely and finally, to rule out all chances of error, to know as well as he knew his own name, what was happening between his wife and John Brown.

Even then, when Elsie had come to help carry the pictures it had been a shock, seeing the light of happiness in her face. It was as though she were being courted by a sunset.

Jim's hurt went so deep that he had needed to claim a headache. This served him well during the ordeal of supper, when he sat with hand to brow and head lowered so he wouldn't have to look at his wife. It didn't cut off the bubbly flow of her talk, however.

Jim couldn't remember ever having heard Elsie go on so. But he knew that it was one more sign of the involvement with John, alongside her help this evening, her springtime opening of the pitch, her avoidance of sex, her oddness lately.

Not until after supper, alone, Elsie making pastry in the

kitchen, did Jim start to mourn. He felt inklings of the grief that follows shock like a shadow. Els, his Els, wife and partner for so many years, was in love with another man. She no longer belonged to her husband.

Jim mourned, a fist pressed over the small white coffin of emptiness in his chest. He was too sorry for himself to feel sorry for Elsie, despite recognising at a distance, like a dog that sees a cat it doesn't want to chase, that his wife was lost, her love sentenced to be unrequited.

Jim knew that John could, in fact, be considering moving on. In which case, Elsie would possibly follow.

That John had not committed suicide, another woman having fallen in love with him, gave Jim a measure of jeery comfort—in spite of his previous conclusion that this would be the case. And suicide came back into his mind with force once he had accepted (his grief holding at the hope of salvation) that the sole solution to this tragedy was for John to die.

Jim left the matter there, retreating nervously in his mind while physically getting up to snap, "Elsie?" His wife answered from the kitchen. He told her he was going to bed with his headache. She called, "Okay, hon. Sleep well."

Red in the eyes because Elsie hadn't come out with hands poised for ministering, body feeling the mourner's exhaustion, Jim went into the bedroom and undressed. Under the sheet he curled up small with only the center of his face not covered.

For a while Jim dwelled with longing on patronage and Venice. He also felt nostalgia for the minor problem of Missy. Then he thought salvation. Tongue hard behind his bottom lip, he concentrated on the crisis.

Immediately, shaking his head in a quiver, Jim agreed that he could not, naturally, kill John Brown himself. He was not the type. He was incapable of anything so barbaric. He could hardly kill a rabbit, let alone a human being. Nevertheless, John had to die.

Jim, who had once marched in protest against capital punishment, had no trouble in acknowledging that it was only fair for John Brown to forfeit his life. After all, he himself had personally taken the life of a man, in Paris, never mind that he had been the cause of many deaths, was about to break up yet another happy home, and was very likely a member of that murderous gang the Ku Klux Klan.

Jim threw in telling factors from both sides of the fence, a round-headed cavalier. His blending of lefts and rights bothered him no more than it would a skilled boxer. A part of his life more precious to him than he realised was being lured away, perhaps occultly, and he believed that reason was on his side, as do devoutly believe all belligerents.

Because he had to, Jim now became convinced that John Brown had meant it completely when he had said he would take his own life if one more woman gave him her love. Elsie, obviously, was a special case.

Not being the dramatic and demonstrative type of female Elsie posed no threat, Jim offered, and when he found nothing further to strengthen his brief he supposed that yes, quite, Elsie had put John on the brink. She had him debating whether to jump or not to jump. All he needed was a little encouragement.

Salvation could be reached, therefore, by following through with what he had been about to do some hours ago, Jim saw. He would feed the philandering, homicidal, racist freak another victim.

Hurriedly amending, Jim explained to himself that Missy and Store Marsha wouldn't really be victims but would only seem to be. The love they would suffer from their second sighting would stop with the death of John Brown, who would be killed by the Gift.

Jim pushed the sheet back from his face. Tongue still, he went over the scenario of what he would do, in two or three days, Elsie out of the way, down at the pitch. It played, he assured himself, professionally.

Some time later, while Jim was playing his scenario for a fourth time, still refining, Elsie looked into the gloom-sad room. She said, "Don't forget, I'm going into town tomorrow morning with a couple of the girls."

"Fine. I'll grab a sandwich."

As Elsie talked about what she and the girls aimed to do, Jim figured how it could have been. The second time she saw John Brown was by accident. The first time was when she went deliberately to his cabin on nothing more than a whim, seized by curiosity. She was like that.

"And the usual stuff," Elsie said.

Jim said, "Have a nice time."

"Sleep well."

"I'll grab a sandwich, I guess."

"Good night," Elsie said. The door closed.

Jim resnuggled his head from having looked up. He released the hold he had on his flicker of excitement. Rather than let it flame stronger by nurturing its spark, the bringing forward of plans to tomorrow morning, he dwelled with satisfaction on how neatly the crisis was working out. That, he knew, meant he had made the right decision.

NINE

The knock woke Missy out of her dream because the cat she was stroking should have been mewing, not knocking. She rolled over in bed, realised she had a hangover, gave the groan of a wealthy invalid.

The knock came again. It was on the cabin door. Sliding out of bed Missy went to answer, a beginner on skates. Since in Shank hangovers were shown off like clean children, not hidden, she groaned again and added, "God, my head."

"Mine too," said the voice of Rachel.

Missy sagged against the closed door. "What's time?"

"Ten. Thought you might be hung so I fixed Bloody Marys. Come on over."

They had stayed in the bar until asked to leave, Missy remembered while she was recognising that lately Rachel had become something of a clinger.

It was understandable, Missy allowed. People on their way up always had hangers-on, which wasn't always good. They could hold you back. There came a time when you had to stop being so big-hearted and think some about yourself. After all, life could end any time.

"Listen, sugar," Missy said.

One minute later Rachel had gone to Bloody Mary it alone and Missy was back in bed. But she couldn't stay there now she had been awakened.

Puffing out her cheeks at Rachel's lack of sensitivity,

Missy got up. After aspirins and coffee she took a long shower. Dressed, she felt fine, free of pain and twitches and the clammy hand of remorse. She felt so fine that she decided to do what she had all along known she would do anyway, be seen in the bar to have a hangover.

Missy had forgotten the oddness of early last evening until she saw Jim. He was coming down the lane as she set off from home. What she first thought of, tutting, was the nuisance, all that climbing for nothing.

When she got within hailing distance of Jim she called out, "Some fun."

"Sorry," he said. "One of those things."

"You acted real strange."

"Strange situation. It'll be different today."

Separated by six feet, they stopped. Thinking he looked every bit as tense as yesterday, Jim, and wondering if maybe he always looked this way but she had never noticed it before, Missy asked, "Today?"

Jim shook his head as though bored. "You don't have to come if you don't want to."

"Gee, thanks."

"I thought I'd let you know anyway."

"Okay," Missy said. "So what was the strange situation yesterday. You looked as if you'd seen a ghost."

Jim laughed as he turned to start back. "Going up. Furniture on the third floor."

Because she wished she could come out with things like that, Missy felt hot on her neck. She said, getting into step at Jim's side, "I don't suppose there's any sense in me asking if you've talked to Elsie yet, about us."

"Not precisely yet, no."

"Of course not. I'll have to be the one to do it in the end, I can see."

"As it happens," Jim said, "I'm going to speak to my wife this evening."

"What are you going to say?"

"Christ knows. I'll think of something, though. I always do when the chips're down."

"I bet you're worried about it."

Jim's concurrent laugh muffled his answer, which in any case sounded to Missy like one of those clever obscurities that she wouldn't understand and would worry about afterwards, feeling dumb. "Be that as it may," she said.

"Right."

"So what was the strange situation up there yesterday?"

"It sure must've looked peculiar."

"You gave me a real workout for nothing. Jesus."

"I'll tell you what happened," Jim said.

John Brown was a passionate birdwatcher, Missy heard as they walked up towards the hardtop. He had been intent on a rare species of thrush when Jim had gone up the last flight of steps. John's frantic signals for silence had sent him down again.

"That's not so strange," Missy said. "You could've told me right then. You could've told me exactly what was going on."

"Well, I was excited. Incredibly rare, that thrush. I had to hurry back to help out and everything."

"It's just not so strange, that's all."

"You don't understand the unusualness of the situation."

Dull as a waterdish Missy asked, "John Brown's not famous for being a birdwatcher, is he?"

"I guess you could say that. But today there'll be no birds. That sighting was an accident, a wild coincidence. It's not likely to happen again."

"I have a hangover."

"You don't look it. You look terrific."

By the time Missy finished telling about last night, making no mention of Rachel, they were standing outside the store, Jim swaying his weight from leg to leg.

He said, "I have to collect Marsha. She's going along."

"She is? Up that climb?"

"We're going to stroll around the long way."

"Well, okay then," Missy said.

John awoke at noon, chill, body stiff from the hard ground, cheek itchy from the sack pillow. Until his mind became clean, he sat staring at nothing while holding his ankles for the comfort.

Physically, John felt near-normal. In spirit he was calm. The sleep had been decent to him, he knew, soothing his muscles and allowing him to digest that, for good or bad or neither, nothing, the deed was done. Whatever happened next, he had not failed. That was quite an achievement.

The whatever next, John mused as he got up, had many facets. The choice started from being arrested for murder and finished with owning the ability to make the woman of his desire fall in love with him. It was as wide a selection of choices as it was possible to reach, a nightmare to a prize, the grotesque to every man's dream of perfection.

Cautiously John left the toolshed. He went to the back door of the house and knocked, the while noting with satisfaction that the burial spot had a natural appearance. There was no response from inside. He left the garden.

People everywhere, John felt safe outside his role of deliveryman. He even drew a measure of complacency from the casual way he stopped, lifted one foot at a time to a car bumper, and rolled down his trouser cuffs.

In heading for the nearest Metro station, however, John was aware that his every move might be under observation. It wasn't a melodramatic or far-fetched possibility. The observers could be gamester psychologists whose interest in his behaviour was clinical, others who were amused by a fool who believed he had killed a man and was expecting a supernatural reward, criminals who wanted to watch the progress of their unpaid assassin. That the police could be involved in an observing way John doubted. They didn't play that kind of game.

He came to a grubby Metro station into which streamed midday people, the harried and hungry. The newsstand inside hadn't yet gotten the papers, though that they would arrive momentarily was made plain by the vendor's glare of scorn at a suggestion that lateness was feasible.

John waited. He bought a ticket for a train that would take him near his pension, he kept aside out of the bustle but not so acutely so that he was conspicuous, he tried to adopt the manner of someone waiting in boredom for a friend who was sure to be late.

In the mirror of a cigarette machine John was let down to see that he looked not sinister but vaguely pathetic. His hair and clothes were messy, he had red eyes, stubble dirtied his chin, and where he had been rubbing one cheek there was a rash.

In a swirl of extra activity, like the star's arrival backstage, the newspapers were delivered. When the first flush of sales was dwindling, John went over. His copy of *Le Monde* he leafed through on his way down to the platforms.

On a rearward page he read without emotion about the unidentified man who had been found dead, apparently shot, in a doorway on rue de la Buanderie. The short item reported in flat fashion, as though it would prefer to be telling of more vital matters. The victim was aged about forty, had no papers or clothing labels. Police were pressing their investigation.

On the platform John read the item again. Wondering, as a passing detour to objective thought, if the matter would have made greater editorial prominence if it had happened on the Champs Élysées, John folded the newspaper. He dropped it in a wastebasket while tightening his mouth with a pull of guile.

So, he finally pointed out to himself, slowly, like one old man to another, the killing had been real. A real gun, a real bullet, a real corpse. He had killed a living person. Furthermore, if the police traced him down as the assassin and could prove it in court, he would spend a lifetime in prison.

John was still thinking of that when a train came trundling in and he felt a hand touch his arm. The shriek of his nerves steeled him into being able to affect a steady turn. He coughed to cover his gasp of relief.

While performing a smile at the familiar face, while exchanging the same vapid well-mets, John was trying to place the woman. American, middle-aged, plain, dowdy, charming.

She mentioned a consulate. John said, "That's right, Mrs. Wilson, we haven't met since then. Nice party."

They talked of changes in the American community, John giving the larger bite of his attention to the train as it stopped, hissed back its doors, let out various of its people. Others began to board.

Gesturing, John asked, "Is this one yours?" The woman, he saw with a throb of surprise, was staring at him. She said, "No." He said, "It is mine." She said, "Please don't leave me."

With Marsha and Missy coming along behind, Jim went around the lane's last bend. He moved like a man who hadn't yet decided which wife to sell to make the least trouble. As he had done regularly, he glanced back with an encouraging call.

Although tense, pale as a groom, Jim was waxing in spirit and convinced he had a tyrant hand on the situation, since he wasn't about to allow disagreement, a change of plans. He was satisfied with progress, felt his behaviour lacked suspicion, liked the way he had handled Missy earlier. All signs pointed to the scheme working out fine.

Ahead, the three cabins came into view on the right, homey and picturesque. Jim gave them the acknowledger's nod. Shank wasn't exactly Venice, he allowed, just as a roadside pitch was no New York gallery, but neither was the village some crumby suburb, and everyone knew what an adverse effect patronage could have on a person's art.

Nearing the first cabin, his home, for the first time it occurred to Jim that Elsie's shopping trip might not be genuine. It might be a cover. She could be meeting Brown in town, perhaps in a motel.

Jim smiled like a baby with wind, which he saw as toughness. Likewise, his taste of nausea he blamed on the fact of realising that if Brown were in town he could not therefore be at home and all this arrangement would not only be wasted, but ruinous. It might prove impossible to get the girls up here another time. The whole scheme would have to be abandoned.

Jim asked himself if he didn't have enough on his mind without having to consider the might-be problems. He asked himself what kind of an idiot was he anyway.

"You're sure this is going to be okay?" Marsha said again just as Jim was looking back to give one of his calls. This time he couldn't pretend not to have heard, she was so loud.

"Sure sure," he said. "You two're special guests."

Missy said, "You said it was a surprise for him."

"It is. You're guests in a different way. He's been wanting to see you ever since the last time."

"So you said. To apologise."

Jim, walking semi-backwards, nodded. "You know what to do?"

"Don't tell us again."

Marsha said, "Seems so far on a warm day."

"I think he has presents for you," Jim said.

Missy snapped, "What's he got?"

"No idea."

"Not something to do with birdwatching, I hope."

Marsha asked, "Birdwatching?"

While Missy was explaining, Jim, walking on, was both telling himself the story, sounded ridiculous, and listening to the growing rumble of a car. The latter becoming a nag, he stopped and turned.

"That car's coming up here," he said.

Missy asked, "Guests?"

Jim answered, "Yes." He would have given the same answer to almost any suggestion, for he needed to be positive and to have an excuse to say, urgently, "Let's get out of sight." The car, which he disrelished with the violence he reserved for all mysteries, could be bringing John Brown back from somewhere, he thought. If Brown saw the women he would do a fast retreat.

By darting back, grabbing a hand of each and towing, Jim got Missy and Marsha behind the Braddock cabin. The three stood there looking untidy, as though among strangers. When the oppressing vehicle flicked briefly into view, through trees in the distance, they all said, "Taxi."

To Jim it seemed a long day of grimaces and sighs and deflected glances, before sounds told of the taxicab's arrival at, queerly, the front of the cabin. A car door opened. Elsie joked with a man about the fare. The door closed. The car moved off.

Marsha hissed, "That was Elsie."

Jim said, "I guess so."

Missy asked, "What's with this hiding?"

"All would be explained in due course," Jim said in a jocular way to hide his puzzlement. He added, "Let's go."

They hurried on, passed behind the Kuzak place, kept onto the last cabin's rear. Jim put his ear to the door. From inside, silence. Brown would probably be asleep at this time of day, Jim thought, which could only be an advantage, like managing to get out of sight when Elsie turned up. The luck was holding.

With Marsha and Missy positioned one on either side of the door-frame, Jim knocked. He used the established signal—six raps followed by a thud. Nothing happened. He knocked again.

To fight a yawn, Marsha stuck out her lower jaw in a pugnacious twist. Missy confided in a whisper that her hangover was going. Jim knocked a third time.

From inside the cabin came sounds of movement. Jim gave a smile left, a smile right, leaned on the wood as the sounds neared, and the second he felt its solidity ease, pushed.

Hair awry, wearing striped pajamas, John Brown moved dozily back as Jim pushed inside talking brightly and with unplanned gasps about a fantastic something that could be seen out front. With no trouble he turned

Brown around and got him into the living room. Alert for the sound, he heard the back door close.

"Oh, that's Elsie," Jim said, acting a look through the window. "Back in a minute, John. Bolt the door." Next, he was outside and hurrying home.

Her hands out together at waist level like a twigless diviner, Elsie circled the table. She breathed unevenly and she stared as though afraid to blink. Fingers frequently changing their interlacing, she stalked out a ring while trying the impossible: to enjoy her stimulation and to settle from it peaceably.

All the way here, expecting Jim to be home, Elsie had anticipated richly. Her big scene she had played out with the depth of a first lady in a last part. So involved had she become, so emotional, that at one stage the driver had asked if she was all right.

And no Jim, Elsie thought. Why couldn't fate or whatever have a better sense of history, if not simple good manners, so that people could have the grand moments they were entitled to.

On a footfall outside, Elsie came to a stop. She was facing the door. When it opened she ended willing this to be Jim and gushed a smile at him with "There you are."

"Hello."

Elsie split up her hands to flap at air. "Thank heavens."

"What?" Jim said, coming inside. "What's wrong?"

"I'm glad you're here."

Closing the door Jim leaned back on it with his hips and head touching the wood. "What happened in town?"

"I came back alone."

"I saw you. A taxi."

"We sure can't afford it," Elsie said to get that in first. "But I couldn't wait."

"I see," Jim said absently. He held his head as if listening, a spy at the minister's door.

"You look agitated, hon. A bit out of it."

"I'm fine. It's the heat."

"Have we had a drink or two, perhaps?"

"No," Jim said, facing front. "What did you mean—you couldn't wait?"

Elsie said, "To tell you." After which she suddenly, absurdly, felt as shy as on her tiro visits to Shank. While Jim was asking what, tell what, she pulled out a chair and sat at the table, her eyes concerned purely with her own vicinity.

She said, "Maybe you should sit down as well."

"I'm fine, thanks."

Although this was not how it was supposed to be, Elsie persevered. Looking up with a toss of her head that helped show herself an I-don't-care attitude, she began to tell it in parts, starting with how she had succeeded in keeping the secret from everyone, even Marsha.

"You had to be the first to know, Jim," Elsie said. "I'd promised myself that." She told of the trip today and what excuses she had used in order to get away from the others. "They looked at me real funny."

Elsie laughed. She was trying to feel easier, harder. With Jim still solemn at the door she told of her excitement over the past days and of the shock before that when she realised what had happened.

"Was told, I ought to say, hon. By John."

Jim stood erect. "Yes," he said. "John."

"This is going to surprise you."

"Maybe not."

"We've met," Elsie said. "I didn't tell you because I knew you'd worry. You know, the love thing."

"Of course."

"We're the best of friends. He's a darling."

"You've met him more than once."

"Oh sure. A dozen times. We have lovely chats."

Jim frowned. He began, "You're not . . . ?"

"In love with him?" Elsie said. "No, hon, not in the least. I couldn't fall for him if I wanted to. That's how it started."

"You're not in love with John Brown?"

"No, Jim. I just said so. Let me explain why."

Lifting a finger to push it under his bottom lip Jim said a soft "Sure."

Elsie told of being out back that day and seeing a man coming towards her smiling. He had said, "Don't worry, Elsie. Everything's fine. Yes, I'm John Brown but there's nothing to worry about. Pregnant women are immune. You're safe." Elsie had said he was mistaken. John had said, "I've developed an instinct. It's infallible. And you, believe me, are pregnant. How do you do." Elsie had said, "Nice to meet you."

Jim's head was turned to the side again, though he didn't appear to be listening to far sounds. His slight agitation had faded. He was almost motionless.

He asked, "You are going to have a baby?"

Elsie nodded eagerly while leaning forward to comfort the hurt that her news had been given in so ordinary a way. "I'm thrilled to pieces."

"Sure."

"I hope you are, too."

Jim stated, "You're having a baby."

"The doctor confirmed it today. Now I really believe it. Before, I did and I didn't."

"But you can't have children. That's what we always thought."

What we always thought was what I let you think, Elsie

told Jim in her mind. No man wants to know that he's sterile.

While nodding, Elsie saw that she could offer the truism that women often conceived when they felt their marriages come under threat. But she would do it later, when Jim was more receptive and they could go into the matter of threats and Rachels.

"We were wrong," Elsie said. "But I'll save the details. Right now I want to know about you."

"About me?" Jim asked, putting a flat hand on his chest.

"Yes. I want to know if you're happy."

"Oh, I see."

"About the baby."

"Sure."

"Jim, you're going to be a father," Elsie said. On this she realised how completely she had rejected her own suggestion on a recent midnight think, that possibly Jim could be told about Philip. That was out. In connection with a child born of love, perhaps; one from a frivolous lust, never. Only the former framed a moral question, the latter being social, and while either revelation would inflict pain only the former was worthy of it, while the latter deserved no more than a wince.

Jim had stepped forward. He looked agitated again. In a jumbled flow he talked of being delighted about the baby but shaken. He was staggered at the news. It was the last thing he had expected. "And you're not at all in love with John Brown?"

"Not at all," Elsie said. "D'you want a girl or a boy?"

"I don't know," Jim said. He had to go now. "Be back soon." He had to think. He was very happy. "A boy, of course." But he had to go. "Be back."

When Jim had made an awkward exit, Elsie sagged gently. Arms crossed on her chest, she touched the backs of her hands to her cheeks. It felt almost as though it were being done by somebody else.

Trailing after Marsha, Missy walked slowly around to the front door again. They had tried the kitchen door and all the windows, twice, knocking and calling out his name. He was making no answer. He seemed to be hiding. It could only be some kind of surprise, the deal Jim had talked about. That was the only thing it could be.

Missy's body was in a droop of languor, she wore a faint, strange smile and the expression in her eyes was pitched betwixt havenly and chary-cross. Never had she felt so unlike herself, so unable to recognise what state of mind she had fallen into. It was like being in a dream yet not inside the dreamer. The closest she could come was by comparing this state to her first experience of love at the age of fifteen, oak tree to a mushroom. So that much, maybe, she knew. She was in love with a man named John Brown, though whether happily or unhappily she couldn't say. She felt lost. She wanted someone to lift her up above the crowd.

Magnifying, for Missy, this eeriness of being in love with a stranger was the odd behaviour of Marsha. She was giving all the orders, she insisted on staying around here instead of going back to the store, she kept repeating that she didn't believe it, she was the loudest of the two when they called his name.

Now, at the front door, Marsha said, "I don't know why you're hanging around." She had said it before.

"I want to see John."

"You can see him another time."

"So could you."

Marsha said, "He might come out if you leave."

"Don't be silly," Missy said in mild rebuke. "This is important. I have to see him."

"Here's Jim. He'll help me."

Missy ran. It seemed alien to her, running, which added another eccentric layer to the way she felt. Jim, coming at a stride, she met and passed in her run, then circled back and walked at his side, her body playing poor old soul with a favour to beg.

She said, "You have to talk to John for me."

"Where is he?"

"Inside the cabin, I guess. You have to get him to let me in, Jim. Please."

"Everything's going to be fine," Jim said. "What happened?"

"It was all so fast," Missy the petitioner said. "I didn't get a chance to speak. He saw me and went very still. He began to walk to the door. I followed and next I knew I was out front."

"Don't worry."

"He locked the door and wouldn't answer. He doesn't understand, you see. That's what it is."

Marsha called out, "Hello, Jim." She stood with one hand on the door and the other towards Jim, its fingers slowly crawling. "Please come and talk to John for me."

Missy hissed, "She's being silly."

As they stopped near Marsha she fastened her reaching hand onto Jim's shirt pocket. Her face was solemn-sad. She said, "I have to get in. He needs me."

Jim said, "Sure."

Missy told Marsha, "You're being silly."

Marsha told Jim, "I love him."

"Just plain silly."

"I love him."

Gravely and firmly, Jim spoke. He was going to help.

They were both to stay here and not move. Something must have gone wrong but it was all going to be fine. They just had to keep calm and collected.

While Marsha was agreeing, Missy followed Jim to the cabin corner, saying, "Okay. I'll be calm as calm. But please try to be quick. Please. I have to see him." As Jim went from sight towards the rear she added, "He looked so holy."

By the time Jim had gone far enough up from behind the cabins to cross the lane unseen, his emotions had stopped being in uncomfortable disarray.

He was no longer stunned with relief at knowing Elsie was not in love with somebody else, or proud of his potency, or excited at the prospect of fatherhood, or worried about the two women, or guilty over what he had done, or harrowed that he might be responsible for a death, or thrilled because of regaining a distant vista of Venice, or concerned over his wife's health; although each of these contributed to his present person.

Jim was in a state of exultation. His spirits floated on a high of power, drifting like wisps of cloud among the beautiful blossoms of tyranny.

He, Jim Braddock, was in charge of destinies. An eminence of the sharpest grey, unsung, he was a giver of life and a taker of life and a manipulator of the lives between. At last he had arrived at his rightful position.

That being a life-taker was untrue Jim managed easily to ignore. Ages ago, minutes, he had decided despite previous decisions that John would not, of course, kill himself. Jim was as sure of that as he was of knowing precisely where John could now be found.

Jim climbed. Not using a zig-zag, he went as near to straight as was allowed by the trees, which he used for leverage. To his present person the going was easy, like forging a path through a crowd of weaklings. Sounds from the breeze-moved foliage could have been murmurs of praise, with courtiers on the cower for a kind word.

Feeling free of the cabins, though keeping his voice low, Jim called out John's name. There was no answer.

Sulk, Jim thought, pulling a face at how lethally John would be thinking of him right now, and then starting to pink on realising he had no story prepared to cover his bringing of the women. Being followed, that one he felt he couldn't get away with a second time. Jim came down in spirit.

He started to pant with exertion. Again he called out and again got no answer. Eyes alert for the boulder that marked John's place, he struggled on upward. The pine aroma began to fade under the smell of his roistering sweat.

It was not the return of that harrowing possibility which had put a needle in his high, Jim told himself on a peasant level of mind. Nor was he worried that he might never get to Venice. He simply hated the idea that he stood a chance of losing John's friendship.

Fighting the last yards, Jim hugged a tree when his head was high enough to see John, who sat in a slump on his seat pile of stones. On the table pile in front of him lay a gun. He was still in pajamas.

Jim accused, "There you are."

"Yes."

"I shouted and shouted."

"Yes, I know."

"You should've answered me," Jim said, still getting his breathing under control.

"Sorry."

"You all right?"

"I've been trying to do it," John said. He spoke as sparely of emotion as before. "I can't."

With a meaningful nod at the gun for himself, Jim went up. On the level he squatted opposite John with the table between, felt the tremble of his legs, sank forward onto his knees, and then sat on his heels. He said, "Listen."

"It's curious," John said. "I want to do it, to shoot, to die, but I can't make my body do the work."

"Of course not."

"I was sure I could do it."

"You're too intelligent, John."

"Intelligence has nothing to do with it," John said mildly. "Except in reverse. Fools never commit suicide."

"Course they do. Anyone who kills himself is a fool."

John looked at him tiredly. He asked, "Why did you bring those women, Jim?"

"That's something for later. Right now let's see about getting you back down home and in a better frame of mind. Things are going to work out just fine."

"How?"

"We'll talk about that too. I've been thinking it over. I may have an idea."

"I doubt if it's new."

"I thought maybe you could try finding Paul Ganieri."

"Please forget the possible escape routes," John said. "Over the past years I've examined every one. Every one. Till I've ached."

"We'll talk about it," Jim said, feeling depressed and of no use.

John said, "Elsie isn't in love with me."

"I know, I know."

"All right."

"I know everything. The baby, everything."

"You're the luckiest man in the world."

Jim said an unconvinced, "It could be a good world for you as well, John. I mean, you know."

John shook his head with the limpness of a decision chipped in granite. "No. I'm leaving."

"Don't say that."

"It's final, Jim. And I can do it now, with help."

Jim tensed. "What?"

"I can find true peace, if you'll help me."

"Me?"

"You'll be doing something magnificent," John said with quiet animation, his eyes no longer tired.

"Let's go back down."

"You'll be bestowing the finest favour of your life, Jim. You'll be giving another human being the thing he most devoutly desires in the whole of creation. Think of that."

Jim said, "No." He rose to a tall kneel.

Leaning further forward in his slump, an invalid conspirator in pajamas and sandals, John used a whisper to speak of noble gestures and of Jim being altruistic. "I sensed it from the start."

Jim said, "No." He was also whispering.

A mere assistant is what Jim would be, John pointed out. "A helper void of responsibility." There was no danger, nothing to fear, neither at the time nor afterwards. "Wipe the gun, put it in my hand."

Jim whispered, "No." He said it again as now John sank down onto his knees matchingly.

"Yes," John said. "You have the strength."

"I can't."

John held out his left hand in ask. Into it Jim put his right hand because he felt his depression lifting. Stolidly he watched as John picked up the gun and settled it into his damp clasp, saying, "There. You do have the strength."

"John."

"A little assistance," John said. Bringing his other hand into use, he held Jim doubly by the wrist. "A little help." He nodded.

Jim answered the nod by raising his head a fraction, an imperious lift. His force was returning, that float of power. He no longer felt useless, impotent. He was a giver and a taker and a ruler.

"Poor John," he said with the gentle smile of superiority.

"Poor me," John said as he drew the gun hand forward. He too was smiling softly. "You are my body." With the gun barrel inches from his chest he stopped the movement. He squeezed Jim's wrist, saying in a mild tone, "Pull the trigger." Jim pulled the trigger.

At the sound of the shot Elsie pushed up from the table. She had been resting, arms and head, adrift in the halcyon waters of a doze.

For a moment Elsie blinked her tired regret at reality. Her mind yawned over the shot; hunters, Jim, town, her baby. Smiling regret away, a hand to her underbelly for the pleasure of showing off for herself, she got up and went to the door. On stepping outside she saw Marsha and Missy.

That the two women should be there, standing near John's door, was curious enough in itself; what fed Elsie's interest and brought her taut-alert was their attitude. Looking away along the lane to where it bent from view, both women were poised in a stance of expectancy, as though watching a race about to start.

Disquieted now about that shot, Elsie began to go towards the end cabin. Jim's oddness minutes ago came back to her and the women's presence here waxed even more curious, so that without giving herself an instruction to do it she called out, "What's up?"

Like precision dancers both women swung around fast and took one step in this direction. Marsha frowned, Missy threw off a gesture of dismissal. They turned away again.

Puzzled and uncomfortable, Elsie kept walking. She declined to indulge in conjecture on account of being unable to think of a beneficial course for it to take.

When nearing the last cabin Elsie saw her husband. He came into sight along the lane, from around the bend, walking in a dull trudge.

At once the two women began to move towards him. Marsha quickened her pace, drew ahead. Missy made her pace surpassing. Within yards both were running.

Feeling the urgency that drifted back, Elsie herself began to run. She did so while holding a hand under each tender breast.

Jim stopped walking. The two women came to a draw stop a way back from him—as if they feared getting too close, Elsie thought as she arrived behind them. She asked her husband, "You all right, hon?"

Jim looked as though he could not have given the question a fair answer. He looked as though he had no notion of if he was fit or ill, up or low. He had the look of someone waiting to be told the worst while hoping for the best.

Elsie asked, "What's wrong, Jim?"

"I was too late," Jim said. "He's dead."

"Oh no."

"He shot himself. He did it just before I got there. I couldn't do anything."

"John?" Elsie said. "John shot himself?"

"Yes."

"He's dead?"

"Yes," Jim said.

The two women said nothing.

Stricken, Elsie stared at her husband. "D'you know why?"

"We'll go into that later."

"Poor, poor John," Elsie said, feeling pain and heat in her throat. "Poor soul."

One of the women went forward. Taking Jim's arm she said to him in low earnest, "Don't worry, darling. You did your best."

"Thank you."

"Just remember, I love you."

Jim peered at her. She said, "I love you more than anything in the world. I always will."

Moved now by sympathy, Elsie went forward. She said, "Don't, Marsha. Don't say things like that. You're upset."

Marsha went on looking at Jim. Missy, coming to Jim's other side, said, "She's been upset right along, talking silly. I'm the one who loves him. I do, don't I, darling?" Jim looked at her. She told him, "You are my one and only god."

About the author

Mark McShane's previous novels for the Crime Club written under his pseudonym "Marc Lovell" include *Good Spies Don't Grow on Trees, The Spy Who Got His Feet Wet* and *Apple Spy in the Sky,* which was released as the film *Trouble at the Royal Rose.* Under his own name, he is the author of many other novels, the best known of which is *Seance for Two,* which was made into an award-winning film, *Seance on a Wet Afternoon.* He has lived on Majorca for over twenty years.